KISS OR KILL

C.H. Lyn, Tracey Barski

To all the weirdos who don't think they deserve a happy ending, and to the friends who never get tired of telling them they're wrong.

CONTENTS

PROLOGUE A MURDER

December was not generally the time to go for a leisurely walk outside in Spokane. The weather sucked, for one. And two, it was well after dark. Never mind that it got dark super early this far north. But I knew better than most exactly why walking at night was a bad idea.

It was sort of a hobby of mine to creep along through the darkness and keep my footsteps as quiet as possible, hoping to go unnoticed by the one I was following. If there was a category in the Olympics for stalking, I'd definitely be working my way toward gold. I'd be the Michael Phelps of stalking. A stalking wunderkind.

I'm really damn good at it, okay?

Tonight wasn't about training, though. This was the real deal, a legitimate mission I couldn't mess up because this guy wasn't some dummy. He was already tuned for unusual sound and movement, on a sneaking mission of his own. He'd killed before, of course, and I couldn't let it happen again.

Creeping around the corner, draped in darkness and shadow, I tucked my tongue between my teeth. I was aware of every tug and pull of my muscles, of every joint that might lock up and crack if I wrenched it just right. I'd spent a lot of time working on my sneaking skills—it took concerted mental effort to step exactly the right way so that my footfalls wouldn't be heard.

Most men didn't worry about being followed or attacked in the darkness, and it was wasted effort on my part. But it didn't stop me from working my damndest to cover my bases.

In this case, I had to employ every tactic I knew for sneaking up on someone. It was imperative that I not be discovered since the stakes were higher than they'd ever been before. He knew I would be looking for him. Which gave me a bit of a thrill, a jolt of something I hadn't realized I'd missed.

There'd been promises about giving up this kind of life.

"You have to *swear*," Karrie had said, holding up her right hand as if she were the one giving an oath.

I'd mirrored her posture, *not* wearing a lopsided sardonic grin, and promised on her life that I wouldn't stalk or murder anyone ever again. I'd had my fingers crossed behind my back because you just *never know* who might really deserve that grisly end.

I took long, slow breaths through my nose, releasing them out my mouth as I tiptoed, my back against the wall outside the apartment.

A rustling sound in the bush made me stop. Trapping my exhale in my chest, I waited, hoping he would come to me. My pretty face wouldn't be my saving grace this time. That wasn't his jam.

I pulled the tiny bag out of my bra, popping the plastic ziplock open.

And just like that, Machete came leaping out of the bush at the scent of the verboten catnip I only pulled out for special occasions. But, alas, I was too late, and he'd killed again.

He abandoned the dead bird he'd held in his mouth for the catnip, and I remembered that I needed to buy more hand soap because I was about to wash my hands eight billion times.

I scooped the white kitty into my arms and made my way back to the apartment. We had some packing to do.

THE CUCKOO'S NEST

Spending a full winter in Spokane, Washington has made the light chill of a Texas December seem scorching.

I can't complain. It was my idea for us to spend the holiday here. As much as Zoe cares for her parents—well, as much as she's able to—if it weren't for me, it's unlikely she'd ever return to the Turners' picturesque cul-de-sac on the outskirts of Austin. Especially now that she has Machete—or Mac—as a good excuse to not leave the apartment. Of course, that excuse went null and void when Zack offered some of his miles to pay the pet fee with the airline.

The flight wasn't half bad. Zack had a tight grip on my hand the whole time, and I tucked away the little sliver of knowledge that he isn't super into flying. But he did it. For me.

My hand drifts to my inside jacket pocket, fingers brushing against the fabric bag resting there before I return my grip to the steering wheel.

I park the rental car on the curb, looking up at the place I basically lived at for most of middle and high school.

The yard is immaculately maintained, hedges and garden as colorful as they can be in the dead of winter. The house itself has never, to my recollection, been anything but perfectly painted and clean.

Zoe's dad used to be a paramedic, but when her mom opened her own private practice psychiatric clinic, he didn't need to work anymore. As long as I've known the family, he's been a stay-at-home-dad. To Zoe, and to me.

The three of us, my ex-serial killer best friend, my current-true-crime podcasting boyfriend, and my leopard-print-jacket-wearing-despite-it-being-eighty-degrees-self, exit the car.

As I make for the luggage in the trunk, Zoe tackles the job of filling Zack in on the dos and don'ts.

"Napkin in your lap," she says in the same tone she uses to remind me to take off my shoes at the door. "Not on the table. Don't bring up One Flew Over the Cuckoo's Nest, or honestly, any movies with psychiatric patients." She pulls the kitty-case, a bright pink mesh-walled container that matches her sweater, out of the back seat. "Don't mention golf—Griller loathes the waste of water—and if you complain about the food and hurt his feelings I will cut off your ear and Fed-Ex it home so you can't get it sewed back on."

Zack laughs, and I also chuckle at this, knowing Zoe's capabilities for maiming go well beyond ears. The last suitcase hits the ground, and I turn to rescue my lover from any more details that might taint his first impression of my surrogate parents.

"Be yourself, babe." I plant a kiss on his cheek, enjoying the warmth of the blush that flushes his already dark tan complexion. "They're going to love you."

"Yeah," Zoe huffs a breath. "You're already miles better than anyone else she's ever brought home."

My laugh hitches in my throat. True words, but the underlying secret behind them puts me off balance.

It's been over a year since Zack and I started dating. Over a year since I found out Zoe had been sleuthfully uncovering dark and terrible secrets concerning about half the guys I've ever been with. Finding out the extent of her investigative skills paled in comparison to the knowledge that she wasn't just digging up dirt on the men, she was also the one planting them in the ground.

Well, half of them.

I shudder despite the warmth of the Texas afternoon sun. The only decent guys I ever got serious with were taken out by a different serial killer—an evil one. A guy who'd been stalking me for years, killing my chances of a happily-ever-after in between murdering any woman he came across who looked like me.

My history of disappearing men kept Zack at a distance... for a while. But the stalker wasn't fooled by our attempts to maintain a platonic relationship. Even then, I felt something special for my true-crime boy.

Over a year later and that something special has blossomed and grown into more than I could have imagined.

Zoe has killed a lot of men, and no one but the two of us knows.

I've killed one. And Zoe, Zack, the Washington state police forces, and a good 2.4 million listeners of *Armchair Detective* know about it. The stalker can't touch any of us anymore, but a year of therapy still hasn't chased away all the nightmares–though the journaling has been helping.

"Hey." Zack puts a hand on my arm. "You okay?"

"Yeah." I shake out of the worry in my heart of what Zoe's parents will say if the topic comes up. There's no reason to think they've heard the podcast. And no reason to think they haven't.

It's not exactly something they'd have called about. Talk about an awkward conversation. Zoe, Zack, and I already decided not to say anything unless they bring it up first.

"Game faces," Zoe murmurs. "Here comes Doc."

I roll my eyes, and turn to Mrs. Turner with a wide smile splitting my blood-red lips. "Mom!"

I leave Zack and Zoe to the bags and run up the walk to throw my arms around the woman. The smell of cinnamon and browned butter lingers on her long brown curls. She always did like to bake. I think it was to steady her nerves after dealing with traumatic clients.

She takes my shoulders and moves me away, just enough to get a good look at me before she grins some more and pulls me in again.

A second pair of comforting and familiar hands closes around the both of us. Zoe's dad is a good six inches taller than her mom. He's also blond as an elf from Lord of the Rings with dazzlingly blue eyes to match.

Zoe may have gotten her analytical brain from her double-PhD-having mother, but her looks—from the hair to the height—all came from Dad.

"It's so good to see you," Mr. Turner says as he steps away.

Mom turns to Zoe and Zack, standing on the bottom step of the short wooden stairs that lead to the wrap-around porch. She gives my arm a squeeze and tilts her head pointedly at the man I'm in love with.

"This the guy?"

Zoe heaves a massive sigh, exaggerating the weight of the bags. "Yes, yes. This is the magical man who has lasted longer than anyone else in Karrie's life. Can we go set our stuff down?"

I grin at Zack's wide eyes. He's used to Zoe. Used to her calling him Tom (a shortened version of her nickname for him—True Crime Tom), used to her preferred level of cleanliness, and used to her spending time with exactly zero people besides the two of us.

But he's also aware that we didn't come back home to visit last year, so he's probably a bit confused about Zoe's indifference to her parents.

"Well, come on in then," Dad says with a laugh. "She hasn't changed a bit," he murmurs just loud enough for Mom and me to hear.

I chuckle, hurrying to help with the bags. The plan to stay from Christmas Eve until New Years was looking dubious when we had to check all the damn suitcases, but now that we're here... I don't even miss the snow.

"They're something else." Zack turns from unpacking his suitcase into the empty top drawer of the dresser in our little room. "I've never..." His words dangle in the air as he takes on a thoughtful expression.

"Yeah," I say with a smile. I move to him, hands going around his waist as I look at him in the mirror over the dresser. "It's weird, right? Kinda like a sitcom or something."

He nods. "I'm half expecting a neighbor to come over with hijinks afoot."

I laugh. "It's not out of the question. This is a chummy neighborhood."

"Oohh." He winces, turning from the mirror and looking down at me with those kind, intelligent eyes. "I bet Zoe hated that as a kid."

My own eyes widen in emphasis. "Yep. She used me as an excuse to get out of playing with the neighborhood kids a lot."

He raises an eyebrow.

I grimace. "Their parents weren't overly keen on me."

Zack pulls away a little, the furrow in his brow chasing away the amusement. "Why the hell not?"

I give half a shrug and move to the other side of the bed to finish hanging up my shirts in the mostly-empty closet. "I was a rowdy kid. Usually dirty, not great with rules or authority figures, and certainly not above stealing food anytime kids from school let me into their houses."

"Familiar," he grumbles.

The room falls into a steady quiet. I hang up the last item—a stunning black dress lined with green velvet for Christmas dinner tomorrow—and stuff my suitcase under the bed.

Then I sink onto the comforter and gaze around the flowery wallpaper. "This was my room for a bit."

Zack joins me on the bed, folding a leg under him and taking my hand in his.

My smile is a little melancholy. "I don't like sleeping alone, so Zoe offered to get a bunk bed." I chuckle. "Like, she put up the money for it. Didn't ask her parents permission, just found one that would work, asked them to drive her to the store, and handed the clerk a wad of cash."

He raises an eyebrow.

"A neatly folded bundle of cash," I amend. "I was only in here a few weeks. After that, we shared a room when I needed a place to crash."

Zack pulls me in, and I lean against his muscular torso for a moment.

When he speaks, his voice is soft. "I remember the day my brother got me a real bed. Instead of the futon we'd shared when we were little." His ghost of a grin is a sharp reminder that while the person who saved my life when I was a kid is still here, his is gone. "It was a shitty discount mattress." His tone holds pain and humor. "He bought me spider-man sheets."

It's my turn to look bemused. "And?"

"And I was almost fifteen."

My laugh brings one out of him as well. It isn't terribly long before Zoe knocks on the door, her sharp rap distinguishable from most others. We hurry out of the room and follow her downstairs.

The evening is sweet. Lightly uncomfortable for the first hour or so as Zoe and I get used to being back under her parents' roof and Zack gets used to a strange place with strange people.

But he's as outgoing as I am when he needs to be. It doesn't take long for him to talk about steak recipes with Dad, baking with Mom, and when Zoe looks unfathomably bored, he manages to draw her into a chess match with the old wooden set above the mantle.

She kicks his ass, but he puts up a good fight.

When I offer to play winner, she retreats to the kitchen.

"It was a dark day at the Turner house when Karrie here beat Zoe for the first time," Dad murmurs with a sly smile.

"It happened exactly once," I return, rolling my eyes. "But she hasn't played me since." I raise my voice a few notches, looking toward the doorway where Zoe fled. "I bet she'd wipe the floor with me if we ever played again."

Dad chuckles and claps a hand on Zack's shoulder. The two turn away so Dad can show him some landscaping in the backyard.

I feel a presence at my feet. With a coo, I stoop and pick up Mac, cuddling him in my arms as I watch the man I love.

My pants pocket feels heavy. The thick band of tungsten, engraved with the words *We solved the case* is beautiful. He'll like it, despite not being a jewelry guy.

Though, this particular piece isn't in the puka-shell necklace category.

"Still gonna do it?"

I wheel around, earning a yowl and claws digging into my shirt from Machete.

"He has a bell." I bounce the cat, proving my point with a little jingle. "You need one, too."

Zoe's smile is small. Unsteady.

Apprehension sneaks into my heart. "I, uh, I was planning to, yeah."

"Okay."

My lips quirk into a frown. "Okay?"

"Yeah, okay." Zoe squints down at me. "What did you want me to say? Was okay not right?"

To anyone else, her tone would sound confrontational. But I know my friend, and she's genuinely asking.

I puff out a sigh and sink onto the couch. The cat darts away, but Zoe joins me on the overstuffed maroon sectional.

"Okay was fine," I mutter. "I just... I want this, Zoe. I want to put something solid behind these feelings. More than a label."

"A promise."

"Yeah." I can't help the somewhat desperate tone. "Because he's worth the promise, you know?"

"No."

I glare at her and, to my surprise, Zoe takes my hand.

"No, *I* don't know. But you know. And he knows you're worth it, too." She glances out the living room window at the figures talking in the yard. "He'd better."

I smile. "He does. It's just..." I take her hand, turning it over to stroke the perfect pink manicure. "Things already changed so much when I moved out. I don't know..."

"Kar."

I swallow, lips trembling now as I try to avoid letting the tears in my eyes escape. Not crying isn't my forte. Thank goodness for water-proof mascara.

"Look at me," Zoe says.

I obey.

Zoe leans forward, planting her forehead on mine with a gentle bump. "You love him. It's weird. It's gooey. It's gross. But you do. More than anyone you've ever been with."

I nod, the feeling rather odd as her head moves along with mine.

"Nothing you do will ever change us, Kar."

I sniff. "Promise?"

"I promise," Zoe says. She hesitates, then pulls away. "But I'm telling you right now, I refuse to wear leopard print at the wedding. Or," she nearly blanches, "black."

My watery laugh brings a smile to her face.

"Now, go blow your nose."

Christmas day is everything it should be—except for the lack of snow. The food is delicious, the company even better, and my determination after talking with Zoe is cemented.

I slept on her words. Let them stew overnight while Zack snuggled me and the tepid Texas breeze kept us cool enough to want a blanket.

She's right, as usual. Sure, things are different now that Zack and I share a place. But I know part of her enjoys the solitude. We still see each other just about every day, still have movie nights every week, and still share absolutely everything.

She'll be all right. *We* will be all right.

And Zack...

I stare across the table, unashamedly admiring the absolute hotness of the man. His plaid button-up is rolled to the forearm, his hair slicked back, earrings glistening in the candlelight.

He's doing a fine job of keeping up with the conversation, and I've noticed he and Zoe are taking care to draw the focus when one of them starts to lose social battery power. A nice break for me, as that's usually my job with the two of them.

Dessert comes out, a raspberry cheesecake that tastes even better than it looks. My stomach is tense though, the ring in my pocket burning an anxious hole through the fabric.

I was going to wait until we went to look at Christmas lights, but dammit, I want to eat this cake.

And I've been picturing his face for the past two months since Zoe and I went ring shopping.

"Hey, babe?"

Zack looks up, and the others glance at me as well. My cheeks flush. I must have broken in at an odd place in the conversation I wasn't listening to.

Zoe's lips spread into a sly smile.

"Can we talk for a minute?" I dedicatedly refuse to look at my friend. My face is even hotter now.

"'Course." He rises, setting his napkin beside his empty cake plate.

I almost tip my chair and hear a light chuckle followed by curious questions from Mom and Dad as I lead Zack into the living room.

"I was going to wait," I say.

He raises an eyebrow, then puts his hands on my arms. "What's wrong, Karrie? Is everything okay?"

"Yeah, yeah. Better than okay! Things are great. Living with you is great. I feel…" I swallow a lump in my throat. No crying. At least not until I've gotten the words out. "I feel so lucky to have you in my life. You've been…" I hesitate a second.

He pulls me in. "I feel the same way, Karrie. I love you so much."

I laugh, sucking in a breath as my hand goes to my dress pocket. "That makes this a lot easier."

Zack's lips part in a cute way that shows his confusion. I slip my hand into my pocket and pull out the ring.

Bare, no box to hold it, no fancy black velvet. The band is in three pieces, a dark section of black titanium with silver on either side. It looks small on my open palm.

I look up at Zack. "Listen, I know guys usually do this part, but it's safe to say nothing about our relationship has been normal. And I like it that way. I like how abnormal we started, and how strange and interesting our lives are. I've never wanted to be tied to anyone except Zoe. But I want to be tied to you. Connected in a... well, legal way, and ya know... Anyway, will... will you marry me?" I fumble the end, but most of my words came out the way I'd rehearsed.

My blushing grin fades in the silence that follows the biggest question of my life.

Zack's eyes are wide, his mouth still parted, but it seems to be shock more than curiosity or excitement. I didn't get on one knee, but I straighten and take half a step back, uncertainty wracking my gut.

"Did I—"

The words, whatever words I was going to say, are interrupted by a shrill ring.

Zack and I both look at his pocket. His phone is lit up, vibrating through the dark blue denim and letting out a series of shrill beeps. With a glance back at me, he pulls it out, thumb on the button like he's about to turn it off.

But something on the screen makes him stop. His brow furrows, mouth closing as his jaw tightens. He meets my eye.

"Karrie—"

"It's fine." I wave him away, shoving the ring back in my pocket and widening my eyes to dry them out. "Take it. We can talk later." I give the worst attempt at a smile in my life, and then watch as Zack shoots me a concerned look before hitting accept on the call and striding away.

I don't think I saw any regret on his face. But my vision is a bit of a blur. Did I do—say—something wrong? Or did I miss the mark entirely on how much he actually likes me? Or... or...

What was that phone call?

I shake my head to clear it, and then go and join the family for the after-dessert cup of hot-cocoa, pretty sure I won't be able to drink any of it with how horribly knotted my stomach is after that fiasco.

Chapter Two

SECRET SERVICE

True Crime Tom loves Karrie. Anyone who sees them together knows this. Honestly, I barf a little in my mouth because of the reasons I know this. Absolutely no doubts about it.

And yet.

As he rushes out of the room he and Karrie disappeared into after dinner, his face pale, his cell phone at his ear, I can't help but zero in on the furtive look he casts toward me and my parents. My bullshit meter takes off faster than Sasquatch about to get his picture taken.

That kind of behavior has me second-guessing, and the look on Karrie's face sends my protective instincts into hyper-drive, urging me to go balls-to-the-wall investigative mode with murder as a very possible last resort. Because I might like Tom—hell, I would even go so far as to call him my friend—but there is no way I wouldn't plant him in my father's garden right this second if he was about to betray my best friend in the whole world.

I glance at Griller, gauging how he might feel about me disturbing his azaleas in the name of avenging Karrie's broken heart. I doubt he'd relish the idea of his daughter committing murder, but the inevitable fertilizing benefit would probably help him forgive me. Plus, he'd do almost anything for his unofficially adopted daughter.

Doc might not be so quick to overlook my homicidal ways. Probably goes against some kind of oath she's taken. But she also carries a secret mama bear side that has come out before, and I briefly wonder if my extreme methods for taking out garbage might have come from her.

I wait to go to Karrie, figuratively sitting on my hands until I get an official signal from her that she needs comfort or help or she gets over her moral quandary and taps me in to do what I do.

Not the wisest, sure. We don't have anyone to pin it on this time if I were to get caught, and Karrie's name and story are now well-known by true crime enthusiasts who'd surely get suspicious if something happened to Tom.

I scowl as I collect the dessert plates for Doc, acknowledging that Tom is as good as untouchable, even if he does something grievous against my favorite person on the planet.

Karrie comes to help me clean up, her mouth a tight line as she glances back to where TCT has disappeared.

"Kar, what happened?" I mutter under my breath as we shuffle into the kitchen.

Doc and Griller are in the butler pantry, their argument about the correct way to make hot chocolate—"No, Diane, it should be two packs of mix. More rich that way." "No, Hank, that has way too much sugar. You know what your cardiologist said."—audible but proof that they won't be paying attention to us.

Karrie still jolts and casts our parents a look. "I popped the question, but he just kind of froze. And then he got that phone call, and it seemed kinda serious based on the look on his face, so I told him to go ahead and answer, but I might've just shot myself in the foot with that one because now I don't know what his answer is, and, Oh God, what if it's no and—"

I place my hands on her shoulders, the wool of the black Nightmare Before Christmas sweater she'd put on after dinner scratchy under my palms. "What if he says yes?"

She doesn't look comforted, and the ghoulish grin on Jack Skellington's face feels like a mockery. If my Karrie ain't happy, ain't nobody can be happy.

I narrow my eyes, shifting my chin forward as I start to turn, my eyes landing on the cutlery we'd freshly washed post-Christmas dinner.

Karrie's eyes widen, and a flash of determination skates across her face. "Zoe Louise Turner, if you grab a knife, I am going to splash this raspberry sauce all over that pink cashmere sweater."

I gasp. "You wouldn't. I *just* got this."

"And you promised me." She feints with the plate of half-eaten raspberry cheesecake—hers because she'd been too nervous about the proposal to eat much of it—aiming for my newest prized possession.

I don't bring up the fact that my fingers had been crossed when I'd promised. And I also remind myself that I've always held myself to a certain standard. Namely that I only kill truly horrible humans, and Tom—breaking my best friend's heart notwithstanding—has never done anything wrong in his life. I've looked.

And I really can't hold his fear of commitment against him based on his history, which he doesn't know I know about. Nor does he know that I spilled those beans to Karrie. Which, I suppose, should help her feel a little better about his hesitation in answering. But putting yourself out on a limb like that can be scary. Or so I've heard.

"Hot chocolate, kiddies?" Griller's grin is pulled taut, and I guess that Doc won the argument about the ingredients for the cocoa.

I reach for the mug he holds out to me, but Karrie doesn't go for hers.

"Zoe," she says in warning.

"I promise." I give her my best psychopath smile and bring the cocoa to my lips.

She sighs and sets the threatening plate in the sink to take the other mug from my dad. "Thanks."

"You girls have an argument?" Doc comes in holding two more mugs of cocoa. "You sound as tense as me and Hank."

"Dad, are you arguing with Mom?" Karrie asks, deftly evading the question and bringing a flush of color to Griller's cheeks.

"Wouldn't dream of it. No one argues with Diane and lives to tell the tale." He affectionately squeezes Karrie's shoulders while Doc shoots me a wink, like we're on the same team.

"Where's Zack?" Griller cranes his neck to glance over to the front room where Tom's been pacing and talking on the phone.

"He got an important phone call," I inform them dryly, my gaze locked and loaded on Karrie.

She glares like she's willing me to leave it at that. Which I do. If there's anything I've made a habit of, it's keeping my parents at a distance when it comes to most deep subjects in my life. Karrie's always had the benefit of not actually being their daughter to keep the ideal amount of space between them.

"Well, Mom and I will go get the movie set up and you kids can join us when you're ready." Griller, always the best at picking up on gentle dismissals, puts his arm around Doc's shoulders and leads her away. Clearly their cocoa argument is forgotten because she lays her head on his shoulder as they head into the den at the back of the house.

Tom doesn't join us until halfway through the movie—Elf, Doc's favorite— and even then, he's distracted, which means Karrie doesn't relax.

Her leg bounces, made more obvious by her creamy bare knee that peeks out beneath the hem of her black dress. I can tell Tom is distracted because normally he puts a hand on her leg when she gets antsy, and his eyes are locked on his phone screen instead of the TV.

Doc and Griller pretend not to notice. I don't. I stare at Tom with my arms crossed. Karrie gives me warning looks, but I ignore her.

And *none* of it registers for Tom, which tells me there's something major going on with him, and I highly doubt it has anything to do with Karrie's proposal.

I think she recognizes this too because her demeanor slowly changes, and she eventually announces that she's tired and wants to get ready for bed three-quarters of the way through the movie. Tom goes with her.

It would seem too suspicious for me to call it, too, so I bide my time. But my fingers itch to get at my laptop keyboard so I can hack Tom's phone. It's surprisingly easy to do if you know the basics, especially when you're on the same wifi network.

After the movie, I barely get into my room before someone is knocking softly but urgently. I know it's Karrie before I open it, but she doesn't rush in and flop onto my bed like I expect her to, like she's done eight million times before.

"I have to drive Zack to the airport at midnight," she whispers as if we're still teenagers sneaking around under our parents' noses.

I blink. That was not what I thought she was going to say. "Um, what the hell?"

Her expression, already dejected, falls further. "Something really serious has come up, and he has to go as soon as possible."

I wrinkle my nose. "Go where?"

"Home."

"Are you going, too?"

She shakes her head. "We haven't been back here in two years, Zo."

I blink again, my nonverbal version of *So?*

She blows a frustrated breath, making the shorter layers of her dark hair dance. "It's important."

"If you say so." I shrug. "Want me to go along to the airport?"

"No. I just wanted you to know so you can help me come up with a way to make it up to Mom and Dad."

I wave my hand. "They'll be fine. Griller's really into that new hydroponic herb garden, and Doc will be engrossed in the newest article in the American Journal of Psychiatry. They'll be distracted enough."

A pained look crosses her face. "Okay. Well, I'll see you in the morning." She turns to go.

"Hey," I say, making her turn back. "Love you."

She gives me a half-smile. "Love you."

I shut the door with my lips pursed, my eyes landing on my laptop on the bed across from me. Mac is curled up next to it, though he's blinking sleepily at me. A little trilling sound comes from his throat—something between a purr and a meow that almost always makes me smile.

I don't smile this time as I walk forward. I glance out the window. It's the same window I used to scowl out of when Karrie was dating that shithead, Vincent, trying to figure out how to break her loose of him.

I run a hand down Mac's velvety coat. He might've been brazen about escaping my apartment—the one I now live in alone as a happy cat lady eighty-five percent of the time (I miss Karrie that other fifteen percent, but don't tell her I said so)—but he had been pretty shaky on the plane ride down to my parents'. And now, he's behaving as if he's lived here his whole life.

My mother had lamented during dessert that he was as close to a grandchild as she was likely to get—with a slicing look in my direction—while spoiling him with little kitty crunchies for his treat.

She sure has mastered the guilt-trip manipulation that she likely diagnoses as problematic in others' lives in her job as a therapist.

To be honest, I love children. If I could figure out a way to have a child without the aid of anyone else, I'd happily sign up. I'm not sure I'd pass a screening for adoption.

Machete bumps his head against my hand to remind me what I was supposed to be doing, but my mind has already submitted to the compulsion to investigate exactly what has TCT hopping on a redeye on Christmas, and I snatch the laptop.

Looking at his phone for who'd contacted him would've been my preference. I might enjoy all the little steps of investigation, but I don't relish going the long way around. Since I can't do it the easy way, I settle on top of the floral pink bedspread with my legs criss-crossed and start digging to get to TCT's call logs.

While this isn't strictly legal, that kind of thing has never been a major concern of mine. Karrie calls me morally gray, using the label commonly attributed to the love interests in a lot of the romance novels she likes to read. I prefer ethically flexible.

It doesn't take long to get into TCT's phone records. Whoever contacted him definitely isn't from Spokane, though it is a Washington area code. I do a reverse search. Seattle.

Hmmm.

TCT lived his whole life in the Spokane area, but I know he spent some time in Seattle. I took the time to listen to his podcast's backlog over a year ago, back when he'd started investigating Karrie for murder. One of his popular and most compelling series involved some mobsters in Seattle.

I pull up a fresh window and do a search on the Farelli crime family in the Pacific Northwest, finding the case I vaguely remember hearing about on the news, well before it was a topic on *The Armchair Detective*. Some major arrests went down and a shake-up of the organization caused a stir among the residents there.

Quiet since then, though. It might be unrelated, and it's quite a jump to make on my part. But the look on TCT's face is urging me to leave no stone unturned.

My tongue taps lightly against the back of my teeth as I peruse the case information before I move on to other research avenues.

Machete stretches, unsheathing the little knives in his paws and digs them into my leg.

I jerk away, suddenly extra grateful for the hot pink fleece pajamas I got for Christmas from Karrie. They were just thick enough to keep his claws from slicing into my skin.

Scooping up Mac, I plop him into my lap and pet him while I keep reading.

Karrie sleeps in, but I'm practically buzzing with the information I dug up. Especially when I found out this morning that TCT did *not* go home. He's currently in Seattle, and I have a little pin on a map updating me exactly where he is every few minutes.

"Zoe, honey, do you mind not having your phone at the breakfast table?"

I look up from my screen, which I'm holding in my lap like a middle schooler trying to keep it hidden from a teacher. My mother's tone is entirely polite and neutral, and she's giving me a beatific smile—her favorite way to deliver censure.

Maybe that's the reason for my homicidal tendencies.

I swallow my irritation. Doc never complained when I buried my nose in a book on forensic biology at the table. But she's always had an abhorrence of screens, saying they are electronic poison to the human mind.

It's not like I know the areas the little pin on my screen is navigating, so I figure I can put my phone away for the moment. I've already looked up flights back to Spokane, ready for when Karrie says the word.

"Thanks, Lovey." Doc smiles and turns her attention back to Griller, who is talking at length about what he's learned in his research into the hydroponic garden I got him.

I take a breath and tune them out, an art I perfected in junior high, and continue debating whether I'm going to tell Karrie about Tom's whereabouts. She's already sideways about the proposal thing. Maybe he gave her his answer on the way to the airport, and I have no reason to agonize over telling her. If he said yes, then she probably doesn't care much where he is. Hell, maybe he told her he was actually going to Seattle, and my whole investigation is unnecessary.

The thought is mildly disappointing. Life has been a little too ho-hum lately, and I could do with a little intrigue.

If it turns out Tom's into something nefarious... Well, he's my friend, and he's a good guy. I won't kill him. Probably. Not unless it's something really bad.

Karrie sleeps well past breakfast, and TCT is staying in one general area of Seattle. I look up the address. It's listed under a Nick Smith, and I give that name a little search.

There are a lot of Nick Smiths. After an hour of sifting through about half the list, Karrie shuffles into the den where I'm sitting with my laptop. She did *not* sleep well. Her hair looks alright, but her eyes are puffy and her mouth is pulled down at the corners, cradled by lines that belong on a face ten years older.

It's clear TCT didn't give her the answer she was anxiously waiting for, and I remind myself that I won't kill him for that.

Karrie plops onto the couch next to me, and I slam my laptop shut, shielding her from the upset this might bring before she's had a cup of coffee. My arm automatically goes around her shoulders when she leans into me.

Then I hear the alert on my phone that TCT has made a purchase, and I snatch my phone to check it, raising my brows. He's paid a pretty penny to American Airlines. Even for a same-day ticket, it's exorbitant. It's more than double the cost of the two return tickets I was looking at for Karrie and me.

So, he's not returning to Spokane alone.

"Why are you tracking Zack's purchases?"

I jolt, scolding myself for forgetting that Karrie is sitting so close she can read my phone screen.

I wiggle the phone at her, offering a tight grimace. "How do you feel about returning home today?"

Karrie gives me a weird look, like she does when she's hung over and I suggest doing yoga. Or like I give her when she tries to convince me to go to a club with her.

Chapter Three

CAUGHT REDHANDED

Z oe is still working. Still buzzing away with her electronics, digging up secrets and uncovering lies.

Lies told to me by Zack. *Family emergency.* I give myself a mental kick for buying that bullshit when I'm well aware his family is gone.

The flight attendant offers water. Zoe vehemently declines and doesn't let me take one either. Instead she pulls bottles bought from the airport Starbucks out of her bag and hands me one.

"Do you have any idea how often they clean airplane water tanks?"

"No." I offer a quick smile to the attendant, who hides an eye roll and continues on her way.

"Exactly. No getting coffee or tea either. Orange juice or soda are okay, but even still, it's not that long of a flight. Better to get something when we land."

I nod along vaguely. I wasn't planning on eating or drinking anything anyway. My stomach is in knots thinking about what kind of trouble Zack must be in to be lying to my face.

As Zoe would probably say, he'd *better* be in trouble. Because if he's not, then he has no excuse.

I press my head to the side of the plane by the window, ignoring the unhappy tsk from Zoe at me unnecessarily touching another surface. Many a wipe was spent cleaning our little area.

Texas is behind us now, our vacation cut short by my desire to find out what the hell is going on with Zack.

I kept in my tears while saying goodbye to Mom and Dad. They hugged me tight, whispering a request for me to drag Zoe back sometime soon. Despite her belief that they wouldn't be bothered, I can imagine how sad they were about us leaving so early.

Zoe was ready to leave the minute we got there, but the call to solve a mystery would have sold her on abandoning our plans even if she'd wanted to stay. I don't know if she's missed the murder—I don't really want to know, though if I'm honest with myself I think she has. But she's definitely missed the sleuthing. The sneaking around, using that smartest-person-in-the-room mind for something besides reviewing and editing entries for publication in scientific journals.

I stare, unseeing, out the window. Spokane isn't far, another hour and then we're home. And what then? Do

I try calling Zack again? The last three times have gone straight to voicemail.

Why is he in Seattle? He doesn't have family there—doesn't have family anywhere—and doesn't have any contacts or friends I've heard about in the last year of being together.

And beyond that. Beyond all the wildness of a midnight flight and secrets and lies is my burning desire to know the answer to my question. He froze. What does that *mean*?

"Hey," Zoe says, her distracted voice almost inaudible against the sounds of the plane. "He's heading home at least. That means we can get answers."

"Answers," I repeat, my voice monotone. Answers to what? Why he went to Seattle? Why he's going back to Spokane with a tagalong? Why he lied to me? Why he froze?

"Listen." Zoe shifts in her seat, facing me as best she can. "It's TCT. Whatever this is, it's something important."

"Yeah... because there's no way he's—"

"Absolutely not," Zoe says with such certainty I raise an eyebrow at her. "Whatever Zack's issue is, he's *not* cheating on you, Karrie..."

Half a smirk sneaks through my racing pulse and saddened heart at the unspoken words dangling from the end of her sentence.

"Because if he was, you'd have to kill him?"

"You said it," she mumbles as she returns concentration to her screen, "not me."

I sit with that for a few minutes. She made me a promise last year that she'd stop her—admittedly well-intentioned—serial killing. It was my way of telling myself it was okay to keep it a secret from Zack. She wasn't doing it anymore, we put a really bad guy in the ground, and no more grizzly deaths were following me.

I heave a tired sigh. "He hasn't told me about the divorce yet."

Zoe closes her tablet.

I glance at her, happy we have the row to ourselves on a relatively full flight.

"Really?" She frowns. "I thought he'd have said something by now."

"Me too." I hug my arms, the black sweater not keeping me as warm as I'd like. "It's been a year, and he knows *all* the shitty background of my love life. I don't get why he'd keep it from me still. Do you think that's why he didn't answer?"

Zoe shakes her head. "He didn't answer because he got a mysterious phone call. As far as the divorce goes…"

I raise an eyebrow at the way she trails off. "What?"

"Well, you're keeping a pretty big secret from him, too."

I purse my lips. "That's true, and also completely different. I'm doing it to keep *you* safe. Who would he be keeping safe by not telling me he was married for all of five minutes when he was nineteen?"

Zoe shrugs. "I won't pretend to know. But, as good at digging up dirt as I am, there are always things the internet can't find. Keep that in mind."

I exhale another sigh, the tense knot in my stomach grinding against my insides.

Zoe slips her fingers through mine and holds my hand for a while. Eventually I try to sleep but am unsuccessful.

The rest of the flight is uneventful, as is disembarking, baggage claim, and Ubering to Zoe's apartment. We opted out of paying for parking because this trip was *supposed* to be over a week long.

It takes barely a few minutes for Zoe to dump her luggage and get Machete settled, then we jump into my car and speed the five minutes it takes to get to the apartment I share with Zack.

"Are we beating him back?"

Zoe glances at me from the passenger seat. "Not by a long shot. His return flight was only a few hours after he landed in Seattle."

"So he's been home but hasn't called or answered the phone."

She winces. "Yeah."

My grip on the steering wheel tightens. "Great." My jaw is tight, the blistering bounce between sad confusion and angry betrayal making my head spin.

The car screeches to a stop at the curb. I usually park in the two story garage next to the building, but I'm too spun up to take the time to find a space.

We hurry into the lobby, and I jam the elevator button with vigor.

The doors open, then close behind us, and Zoe turns to me. "Remember, we don't know what we're walking into. Caution and patience."

I inhale through flared nostrils. "Caution if he's in trouble and patience because if you kill him today it'll be way too obvious, and we'll both go to jail?"

She smiles, reaching out to squeeze my arm. "You know me so well."

\#

The door isn't busted down, but it is locked. I slide in my key as quietly as possible, turning the knob and pushing the door slowly while Zoe gives comforting nods and keeps her hand on my shoulder.

We tiptoe in. My stomach lurches at the extra bag in the living room. Not a suitcase, but a thick and dingy backpack. Zoe's nose curls at the sight of it dirtying my pretty sitting room rug.

The layout for this apartment isn't my favorite, but it was a good price and less than ten minutes from Zoe—which was my make or break for everywhere we looked.

The sitting room is open with wide windows across from the door and plenty of space to push aside the coffee table for a quick yoga session in the morning. Instead of immediate access to the kitchen, there is a swinging door that leads to a long hallway which then leads to the kitchen, bathroom, office, and bedroom.

It's from the swinging door that we hear voices.

Men's voices. One clearly Zack, and the other a stranger.

Zoe crooks her finger for me to follow and leads the way, padding silently across the floor—when did she take her shoes off?

I slip out of mine and obey her directive, avoiding the spot where the wood squeaks as she carefully pushes open the door to the hall.

Lack of a barrier increases the sound quality, and my throat goes dry at the words we hear.

"I'm telling you, we need to talk about this." Zack's voice is steady, but there is strain in his tone.

There is a brief pause.

"Get out of my way," the stranger says.

Zoe and I exchange an alarmed look at the cold, gruff voice.

"Come on, Nick." My boyfriend sounds almost exasperated, but cold seeps into my stomach.

Zoe and I inch forward.

The gruff stranger speaks again. "I will pull this trigger. Move."

"*No!*" I wanted it to be a shout, but my cry comes out more like a squeak as I lunge into the kitchen.

My face flushes at the sight before me.

Zack stands in front of the microwave I'd meant to clean out before we left for Texas. In front of him, facing slightly away from me, a tall, broad shouldered man with shoulder-length brown hair has a bottle of all-purpose spray in one hand and a damp rag in the other.

Both men turn to stare. The stranger takes a step to the side, blocking Zack from my eyeline for a second before my boyfriend moves around him and hurries over to me.

I flush further. Little pins and needles crawl up my arms as embarrassment hugs me. "Sorry, I thought—"

My eye twitches.

Zack looks at me, eyes wide. "Karrie, what are you–" He shakes his head, closing his arms around me. "I'm sorry. I'm sorry I had to leave so suddenly."

I don't return the hug, but I lean into him a little, enjoying the musky scent of pine that sticks to him like sap. When he pulls away, his expression suggests he understands the hot water he's in.

"So." I cross my arms, moving to lean against the far counter as Zoe slips into the room behind me. The kitchen isn't overly large, but a little breakfast nook makes up for the lack of space. The four of us fit fine; it's the secrets making things cramped. "Who the hell is this? And what the hell is going on?"

Zack glances from me to Zoe–who also has her arms crossed and is giving him a deadpan stare–to the man, Nick, who looks back at him and gives a brief shake of his head.

I squint, frustration rumbling in my empty stomach.

"He's Nick Farelli."

The name-drop is followed by silence as Nick, Zack, and I all gape at Zoe.

She lifts and lowers a shoulder with all the nonchalant grace of a prima ballerina. "Mobster, grifter, all around enforcer with multiple aggravated assault charges on his record and a litany of," she does finger quotes, "*excused* traffic violations."

Her expression shifts from bored to haughty, and a burst of pride blooms in my chest. I *love* being besties with the smartest person in the room. Most of the time.

"He was also a guest star on Armchair Detective five years ago. Through the anonymity of a John Doe, of course. Made the case for the feds to arrest his uncle." She turns to stare daggers at Zack. "If I recall correctly."

The man, Nick, stares with narrowed eyes, still silent as the grave. He's quite tall, inches over Zoe, and as intimidating looking as his bio would suggest. The clothes are well worn, but clean and only lightly wrinkled—probably from the flight. A bandage around his left arm draws my attention for a second.

Zack meets Zoe's gaze for a few seconds, then gives a shallow nod before running a hand through his hair. "How, exactly, do you know all of this?"

She grins, eyes glinting like a predator about to strike. "Seattle, mob, podcast... it wasn't difficult to look up mugshots from the people who were arrested in that big bust you had a hand in. One of them *had* to be your informant. I recognized him." She scowls at Nick. "Despite the shaggy hair."

Though I'm still pissed at Zack, I can't help returning the look we've developed over the last year and a half whenever Zoe shows off her impressive sleuthing skills. It's a combination of exasperation and pride, with annoyance occasionally included, though not this time. The look shifts a little as he surveys Zoe. His brow furrows a smidge, like it does when he's trying to figure out a complicated aspect of a case.

After a few seconds, Zack shakes his head, puffing out a breath.

My lip curls at the edge, a smile finally replacing the muted frown I've worn since asking Zack to marry me. "Well, now we're getting somewhere."

CHAPTER FOUR

A MOBSTER-SIZED PROBLEM

"**A** mobster?" Karrie says to Tom, and he grimaces, placing his arm around her shoulders, tugging her toward the living room like he's trying to put distance between her and Nick.

I'm left to size up said mobster. He returns my appraising look, maybe doing the same. I feel a strange sense of territorialism standing here, facing off with him. It's a rare experience, feeling challenged simply by the presence of another person.

Unsettled by the sensation, I turn my attention to the spray bottle in his hand. Not the worst brand on the planet, but definitely not the best cleaner I've tested. And yes, I did buy those tester kits.

Reconciling this gruff-looking man holding a cloth and an all-purpose cleaner is a bit difficult. He's wearing well-loved house shoes like he isn't into walking around barefoot, and there's a pair of nitrile gloves poking out of his back pocket. He's also sporting a suspicious-looking bandage on his upper arm, exposed by the loose t-shirt he wears.

I struggle to engage with this unreadable human. I'm honestly not sure what level of brain function I might find here (my gut instinct is cannoli—pretty to look at and probably tasty, but not much substance), so I reach for the only common ground we might have. Aside from murder, of course.

I gesture to the bottle in his hand. "That brand is only about 78% effective at killing germs."

He lifts it, glancing at the label. "It's all that was available. The girlfriend used the last of the good stuff."

His voice is low and somewhat sinister-sounding. I can see the intimidation factor, though I don't think it's something he actively works at. Maybe it's how he's always been, maybe it's his role in his family's crime syndicate. It doesn't much matter since it gets the job done.

"The girlfriend has a name, you cannoli" I say, my arms still crossed. But the reminder that all those cleaning habits Karrie picked up living with me have hung on, even when she didn't *have* to adhere to the strict guidelines I set up, makes a little spot in my chest warm.

The Cannoli's expression remains neutral. "He never told me her name."

Yeah, maybe for a reason. I'm pretty sure Tom would want to keep Karrie as far from this situation—whatever the situation is—as humanly possible. And since he's reasonably intelligent, he probably never told the Cannoli her name on purpose.

We'll call that little flare inside of me grudging respect. Especially considering that I willingly allowed her to walk right into this potentially dangerous situation. Not that I anticipated him *inviting* a known killer into the home he shares with her.

I spin to follow where Tom and Karrie have disappeared to so I can scold him for the fact.

"—he just needs a place to lie low for a while," TCT is saying.

There's a notable distance between them on the couch. Karrie's not usually into personal bubbles—as in *honoring* them. Tom has never seemed to mind. Since they started dating, there's hardly been breathing room between them, much to my dismay.

But this throws me off. The Cannoli-sized chasm that separates them is only widened by the as-yet-unanswered proposal that hangs in the air and weighs Karrie down like a backpack full of rocks.

Her eyes shoot in my direction, but I'm pretty sure it's because the Cannoli has followed me out of the kitchen.

"Why exactly does Nick Farelli need to lie low for a while?" I ask, though it doesn't take a high IQ to guess he's either gotten on his family's bad side, or he's suddenly on the lam from the feds. In either case, the question would be why.

The Cannoli meets my gaze as he passes me, his expression unreadable, which is irritating. I might not understand people in general, but they're not that hard to figure out as far as emotion goes. If their face doesn't give them away, their body language will. You don't have to get the why to know the what and anticipate accordingly.

And yet the Cannoli moves across the room with a graceful ease that strikes me as mildly dancer-like, the cleaning spray still lightly clutched in his hand. He seems unfazed by this entire situation. He didn't even look that startled when Karrie burst into the kitchen to save Tom from death by antibacterial cleaner.

"Someone sent an enforcer to take him out."

"And he called you?" I deadpan. "Don't get me wrong. Tom's a smart guy, but I wouldn't exactly file him under bodyguard material."

The Cannoli looks back and forth between us, eyes narrowed. There's definitely a level of dangerous suspicion that edges his gaze. "Who the fuck is Tom?"

I gesture at TCT, knowing it's not an obvious answer but feeling annoyed about it, anyway. "True Crime Tom."

The Cannoli's eyes narrow further.

"Nicknames are her thing," Karrie says, rolling her eyes.

Tom, to his credit, doesn't look offended. Karrie, however, shoots me a *really?* look.

"He didn't call me," TCT says, redirecting the conversation. "Someone else did. I got a tip that Nick was in danger, so I jumped on a plane to warn him."

"Why?" Karrie asks, her dark eyes sliding to the Cannoli like he's a poisonous snake.

"He doesn't have a lot of options for who to trust right now."

I file away TCT's intense sense of responsibility for the Cannoli under *to be investigated.* "So on the outs with the family, then."

The Cannoli sets the spray bottle on the table in the dining room portion of the space and looks at me. "You're used to being the smartest person in the room, aren't you?"

I tip my head as a little blossom of heat forms in my chest and radiates through my veins. A stillness takes over my body, and I'm very aware of the way Tom and Karrie are watching me.

"Am I wrong?" I reply, my voice deadly calm. I see Karrie flinch in the corner of my eye, her gaze shooting to Tom as if he might suspect something. As if he would guess I'm a killer based on this interaction. It's not like I'd resort to murder for someone being sassy with me. It is tempting, though.

The Cannoli shrugs.

I stare at him for a long moment, and he keeps my gaze unflinchingly. A weird feeling stirs in my belly. Irritation, annoyance, a little thrill that confuses me. Like there's a part of me that likes how he's challenging me. Which then makes sense, given how I thrive on challenges. This mafia cannoli is simply a complicated math equation. Explains my irritation as well.

Tom clears his throat when the silence stretches tighter. "The problem is we're not sure where the tipster is."

I turn to him, though the Cannoli keeps his attention focused on me.

"What do you mean?" Karrie sounds a little panicked, her inability to keep herself from touching TCT obvious in the way her hand has found its way into his.

He squeezes it as he answers, "I was supposed to meet with him first. He didn't have exact details, but he knew the hit on Nick would be soon. I was going to meet him to get more information, see if I could suss anything out that he missed. That's why I had to leave so suddenly last night."

That explains the abrupt departure, but not the lie about why, and I squint in his direction. Karrie gently extricates her hand, clearly thinking the same.

"Then he didn't show for our in-person meet. So I went to Nick. Good thing, because someone had him in their sights already." Tom gestures to the mobster, the bandage on his arm now making sense.

"Oh my God, Zack!" Karrie says, going predictably green at even the roundabout mention of blood.

"Just a graze," the Cannoli intones casually.

Tom winces. "That convinced him pretty quickly that we needed to leave town."

I toss the Cannoli a hooded gaze. "Yeah, I'll bet."

He tucks his tongue into his cheek, looking like a sullen teenager having his dirty laundry aired out.

"Who's the tipster?" The question comes from me, but I'm watching Karrie closely. Her green pallor has changed to an off-white that has me concerned. I don't think we're in danger of eliciting her famed death talk-induced vomiting habit since no death has been explicitly mentioned, but she is not handling this news well. Being mixed up with mobsters, even loosely, is pretty unsettling. Not a decades-long-stalker-kills-any-man-I-get-close-to unsettling, but it's a close second.

"Stretch."

I look at the Cannoli. He's still by the table, his stance squared, but his hands are in his pockets. I decide that even though the hair is shaggy, it's a look that works for him, the black locks curling at the ends at just the right place to make it seem intentional.

"Stretch," I repeat dryly, sharing a look with Karrie, whose eyebrows quirk.

"A cousin," the Cannoli adds, a slight smile tipping the corner of his mouth.

"So that's why you think the family is responsible?" I ask.

"Seems likely." The Cannoli adds a little shrug for emphasis.

"It's not like you don't have your fair share of enemies," I point out.

"Stretch said it was a direct order from someone at the top," Tom replies. "I took that pretty seriously."

"But you don't know who ordered the hit?" Karrie asks, rubbing her arms as if she's chilled.

"Nope." The Cannoli pops the "p" at the end.

"And Stretch is trustworthy?" I direct this question to both of them, but I'm still looking at the Cannoli.

"Usually." No waster of words, this one. He must know it's annoying, particularly to me.

"He's always been a good source of information ," Tom offers helpfully. His tone is entirely too bubbly. Because this is his passion—the methodical poring over facts. "When I was doing research on some of Seattle's crime families, Stretch was my main guy. As honest as they come—so long as you're not a cop."

I give him a dubious squint. "Well, as trustworthy as Stretch is, he's now *missing*, right?" I give Tom a significant look, my eyes dancing to Karrie for emphasis. "So that means we've got an unknown villain hiding in the shadows. Again."

Tom's eyes widen as the accusation settles. Karrie's face pales a second time.

"But since we're not involved in this little mess," I continue. "I think Karrie should come home with me, and you boys can have your sleepover and braid each other's hair or whatever. His is long enough." I toss my head in the Cannoli's direction and look to Karrie for confirmation. I use a very tight stare in her direction to telepathically remind her that he ran out the door on her right after she proposed and *still* hasn't given her an answer.

She nods, the message successfully landing. She stands to join me.

"Isn't that the reason you lied to her about where you were going in the first place?" I fold my arms across my chest, and Karrie mirrors my pose. The topic had sort of taken the wind out of her sails, but she's a gathering storm again.

The Cannoli smirks, but he says nothing as Karrie and I turn for the hall that leads to the front door.

TCT jumps to his feet. "Wait, that's not—"

I hammer a glare in his direction, but it's Karrie who speaks: "You know I love you, Zack. But I've left my dealings with lying men behind me." She shoots me a nervous look, but I don't acknowledge it. "I think Zoe's right."

We head for the door again, and TCT trails behind us. "Well, can't we talk about this?"

"Sure," Karrie tosses over her shoulder. "I'll call you."

TCT stops dead in his tracks halfway down the hall and watches us leave.

CHAPTER FIVE

UNWANTED BRUNCH GUEST

My temper cools by the next morning. Partially because I don't hold a grudge like Zoe does, and partially because my stomach is grumbling too loudly for me to focus on anything else. And a little because I woke up at 4am, couldn't sleep, and spent an hour scribbling notes into my black leather journal. It's filling up. Fragments of thoughts, memories, various lists.

Zoe makes a mean scramble, but given everything she's already done for me in the last few days, I have a striking desire to treat her to something nice.

I'm already up earlier than usual. That, combined with the sun's winter track, means the light outside is limited to a dim gray glow along the horizon. I tug my hat lower and zip my jacket all the way to the top.

The car takes several minutes to warm up. While it does, my stomach grumbles again, eager for a meal large enough to make up for skipping dinner last night.

Zack's lie sits on my chest, constricting my airflow and driving a fresh bolt of frustration through my gut.

I grit my teeth and zip out of the parking lot. It's too cold for windows down, but I blast my music just the same, the vibrations helping to pull me out of the rut of sadness that comes immediately after the anger.

It doesn't take long to get to my favorite brunch house. I park at the front and frown. There's something different about the building. It takes me a full twenty seconds to realize the lights aren't on.

I glance at the car clock. The restaurant doesn't open for another twenty minutes.

I slump in my seat with a groan. There is something hurtfully special about the level of stupidity, foolishness, and frustration I feel.

This is not how the holiday season was supposed to go. A new year is right around the corner, and rather than facing it with my usual level of optimism and excitement, I'm stuck in a weird limbo, bouncing back and forth between being furious at my boyfriend and immensely concerned because a real-life mobster is staying in our apartment.

I scroll the goth side of TikTok for a few minutes, making a mental note to try out a delicate spider web eyeshadow design. Before long, the lights flick on and a figure wearing an apron flips the sign on the door from closed to open.

I scurry inside, my jacket fighting the frigid air until the door closes behind me. The barista offers up a warm smile which I return. I place my order—two large lattes, two croissant sandwiches, and half a dozen pastries—and settle into a corner table to wait. The kitchen has probably barely started their burners, so I imagine it'll take a while.

I tuck a headphone in, leaving one ear open like Zoe prefers me to do when in a public space. I get busy-work done. Check stocks and account information for my personal stuff and Armchair Detective (angry with Zack or not, I've taken over most of the paperwork stuff for the podcast, and I'm not going to shirk my duties).

There are a few new comments on the final episode of the *Black Widow Saga*—my saga. The one that ended up not being black widow at all, but the title was too good to not use.

My pulse jumps a little at the new activity on the wrap-up episode. This happens every time we get a new batch of listeners eagerly diving into the story. Zoe and I spun it well. We tied up loose ends and managed to pin every one of Zoe's murders on the man who'd been stalking me since Freshman year of high school.

Zack said there would be people who didn't like how the story ended. We've had a handful of comments questioning how Reginald was able to slaughter so many people before getting caught.

Each time someone comes in with a stick to poke holes in my story, I get a nervous clench in my stomach.

Each time, I wonder if we should've told Zack the truth. Maybe he would've been okay with Zoe's trail of bodies. Maybe he would've had a better plan for covering up the murders.

Not that there was anything wrong with our plan...

I grit my teeth, glare at a fresh comment wondering how neither Zoe nor myself realized someone was following us for years, and exit out of the podcast.

"Karrie?"

I jolt backward. Heartbeat thundering in my ears, my gaze lands on the culprit of my heightened anxiety.

"Nick?" My tone is anything but welcoming. What the hell is he doing here?

"I thought that was you." The mafia man responsible for my boyfriend lying to my face and not giving me an answer to my marriage proposal offers up a tight smile. It looks out of place. Like his lips don't usually move that way.

I stand, shifting my purse from my lap to the tabletop. "Hi. What are you doing here?"

He gestures to the display case a few feet away. "Zack mentioned this place yesterday. I wanted to grab some breakfast to—"

"Thank him for letting you stay at the apartment?" I finish for him. It's less of a question and more confirmation that he's here for the exact same reason I am.

He nods, shaggy dark hair drifting across his face. He brushes it away, a furrow in his brow as he moves the strands.

He's certainly nothing to balk at, as far as looks go. I get why Zoe's appraising eye was stuck on him for a while yesterday, though she's coolly dubbed him the Cannoli. Nick's warm brown eyes glance around the little restaurant.

It's a quiet morning. Not that I'd expect much else in the predawn hours during the days between Christmas and New Year. It's a crossover of liminal times. We stand alone; even the barista is in the back still. She hasn't taken Nick's order yet.

"Is your friend here?"

I raise an eyebrow.

"The... clean one," he elaborates unnecessarily, stumbling over the words a bit.

"No," I reply with a muffled grin. "She's hopefully sleeping in. We had a *long* day yesterday." I also gesture to the pastry case. "I'm in the same boat, getting a thank you breakfast."

Chagrin isn't something I'd have expected to see on the face of a mobster, but Nick Farelli looks apologetically guilty.

"Sorry about all this," he says. His hands dip into the pockets of his well-fitting pants. "I never wanted to get Zack mixed up in any family business."

I'm tempted. So tempted to ask how Zack is. If he slept last night or tossed and turned like I did. If he already misses me. If he's told Nick about my asking him to marry me.

Instead, I keep my focus on the mob-sized situation at hand.

I stuff my hands in my jacket pockets simply to have something to do with them. "Family business." I shake my head. "Did you sort out why someone's after you, yet?"

He shifts his weight, and I take half a step back, bumping into my chair. A cloud of regret seems to hover over his head. His expression makes me feel a little bad about backing up. But only a little.

"No," he says. "Zack did some digging after you left yesterday. The sooner we get this figured out the sooner he can clear the air between you two."

My eyes go wide at the same time that he winces. Heat stirs in my chest. Anger that Zack thinks getting his friend back to mafia business is all it'll take to ease my hurt.

Nick must read the fresh frustration on my face. "Can you... can we pretend I didn't say that? I'm a mess before coffee. My uncle always said I need to watch my mouth in the morning."

I sigh, my anger leaving as quickly as it came. I'm not as good at holding onto it as Zoe.

"Yeah, people say that about me when I haven't eaten in a few hours."

Nick chuckles. "What about your friend?"

I cock my head at the question. "What about her?"

"Uh, does she have any particularly dangerous times of day?"

I freeze for a full several seconds, the wheels in my brain turning slowly, then faster as it clicks that Nick has a *crush*.

I try not to smile and fail. "She's pretty dangerous all the time." Pride and humor mingle as one in my tone.

A bit of pity twinges in my stomach. Nick has no chance with Zo, and not just because he's a mafia man on the run. Despite what her lingering gaze yesterday might have seemed to suggest, I'm well aware she has as much interest in men as dumpster-diving.

He nods, his expression a bit distant.

"Are you close with your uncle?" I redirect back to the reason he's here in the first place.

Nick's distant gaze focuses and darkens. "I used to be."

"Can't he keep you safe, then?" The words stumble out before I can pinch them between my lips. Clearly I also need caffeine before having a conversation with someone without putting my foot in my mouth.

The feeling that I've said the wrong thing only amplifies when Nick's eyes take on a cold air as they meet mine. "No."

He leaves it at that, and we stand in awkward silence for another few seconds before the barista saves my ass by calling out my name. I give Nick a quick goodbye nod, grab my bag and coffee carrier, and zip out the door.

I get back to Zoe's apartment with a burned tongue from sipping my latte too quickly, burned cheeks from my intrusive questions, and burned heart from thinking about Zack the whole drive home.

I eat with Zoe, then retreat to the spare bedroom to curl into a ball with Mac and pet him until I can stop crying.

CHAPTER SIX

BOGGED-DOWN BABYSITTER

K arrie mopes around the house for two days before TCT decides to show up because she definitely *hasn't* called him.

She didn't complain much to me in that time. We carried on as usual, falling back into the routine of living together like she'd never left. The habits are too ingrained to have changed anything between us.

But I can tell she's really bummed, and part of me regrets taking her from our parents' early. At least she might've been distracted there. Doc and Griller would've continued doting on her since I am not receptive to that kind of hovering.

I don't like it when she's hurting, and it takes some artful efforts to distract her, which means my deep-dive into the Farelli family takes a backseat. All I've gotten so far is a list of people in the family who might be our culprit, and little else. As much as I love Karrie, I also love a good mystery, and I'm chomping at the bit to get back to my research.

So when TCT knocks on our door, looking appropriately distraught at the radio silence from Karrie, a flood of relief overwhelms me, and I practically yank him inside before he says a word.

In the brightness of the living room, he looks worse than he'd seemed in the glow of the porch light. Good.

"Kar, someone's here to see you," I call down the hall.

Mac was pulling one for the team and had engaged her in some feline game in my room. I'd heard the giggles and the sound of his claws on the carpet. I swear that cat understands humans better than I do.

TCT is wringing his hands, pacing in the small foyer as we wait for Karrie to walk down the hall to the living room. Her expression is definitely distant as she takes in his slightly disheveled appearance.

"Karrie, I'm so sorry," he starts, working to keep himself from rushing toward her. "I know I messed up, I..."

She purses her lips and puts her hands on her hips. And damn if she doesn't look like an imperious queen. She's even got her ass pants on. It's like she planned this.

I have a hell of a time keeping my grin under wraps.

"Come with me to dinner, and we can talk things through?" He's practically begging.

Her expression softens, and she looks at me. I give her my most subtle look of approval. The freeze-out has been the appropriate length for his lying, and I understand his motivations. I'd kept things from her for years in an effort to protect her. The most I got were incredulous outbursts. And vomiting.

"Okay," she says after a tense moment passes.

TCT noticeably relaxes, and I silently cheer. If it means Karrie won't be so sad, I'm all for it. Plus, it frees me up for what I've been dying to do since we got back.

Karrie grabs her purse, her dark red lips almost disappearing in the flat line I associate with her displeasure. Then TCT turns to me, and I freeze at the intent look on his face like he might know what I'm about to do.

"Zoe, do you mind going and hanging out with Nick?"

I give an exaggerated glance behind me like there might be someone else in the room he's asking. Surely, it isn't me. I don't hang out with anyone—ever—and he knows this.

He grimaces. "I'm just worried about him."

I raise a brow, finding his devotion to someone like the Cannoli a little odd, though it is mildly endearing. Tom is apparently as loyal as he is committed to the truth, and he undoubtedly has no illusions about what the Cannoli does. So that must mean there's something redeemable about the guy.

Blowing out a breath, I reply, "Fine."

It's clear TCT wants to do something like hug me, but it's a momentary lapse in judgment on his part, and he catches himself just in time. Karrie is about the only person allowed to touch me, and that's because she follows hand-washing protocols to the T.

Grabbing my laptop and keys, I follow them out. I might've agreed to hang out with the Cannoli, but my version of hanging out is ignoring him. I'll probably even do my research while I'm there.

I part ways with TCT and Kar in the parking lot, and I've almost forgotten where I parked my car. If I go anywhere, it's usually with Karrie, and she always drives. When I do find it, I'm relieved to find the gas tank is still half-full. Who knows how long it's been since I filled up?

It only takes a few minutes to get to Karrie and TCT's place. Karrie thinks she's sneaky, but I know she picked this complex because of how close it is to me. The sentiment is sweet, and I'm glad she's not far.

Parking in the lot a few spaces down from their building, I start gathering my things for the evening. My lip curls back at the thought of spending my time anywhere but home, especially when Karrie hasn't been there to keep the cleanliness up to snuff. An image of the mobster with cleaning spray and a rag in his hand comes to mind, and I purse my lips, considering.

Just then, my phone vibrates an alert. It's a hit on the search I'd been running on Stretch. My brows rise at the news that might make for an interesting conversation with the Cannoli this evening. Perhaps ignoring him isn't on the agenda.

I've just reached for my door handle when the man, himself, comes striding out of TCT and Karrie's apartment, stilling my movements. He heads for a dark sedan parked opposite of me. Sometime in the last two days, TCT must have gotten the Cannoli a rental car. Or he'd surreptitiously gotten it for himself.

Either way, this babysitting job is turning out to be much more interesting than I'd anticipated.

CHAPTER SEVEN

DINNER, INTERRUPTED

Awkward. Awkward is the only word I can use to describe the drive to dinner. Zack's hands are sweaty on the steering wheel, his gaze darting over to me every time we stop.

For my part, I've managed a very Zoe-like stoicism that is extremely out of character for me. I'm not even holding Zack's hand, though he's put his arm on the center console enough times.

I'd feel better if I was the one driving. Having something to do, besides pretending to look at my phone, would help my nerves.

It's not until he parallel parks a block from our favorite restaurant downtown that I break the silence. Because having the brunt of this conversation at a nice table while a poor waitress tries not to interrupt is *not* the vibe.

"You lied to me."

He winces. "I know, Kar. I'm so sorry."

I shake my head, putting a hand up. The glossy black polish on my fingers glints in the streetlights coming in through the windshield. "Let me finish, okay?"

He nods.

"I get keeping secrets." My stomach churns a little at the words. He doesn't know how true they are. "But lying to my face is different."

He's silent, watching me intently with the car keys dangling from his hand.

My lips twist. "Everybody's got stuff," I murmur. "I know that. But you could have just said a friend needed your help. I would've understood."

He nods again.

I grimace. I want to address the elephant in the car, but the idea of facing my failed—or at least stagnant—marriage proposal is too much for me at the moment.

Besides, I want to get some information about Nick. I know Zoe's been chomping at the bit to dig into everything she can possibly find. It's only me at the apartment that's stopped her going full Sherlock.

"You can talk now," I say dryly.

"I'm really sorry."

I nod. "I know."

His creamy brown puppy dog eyes widen, a glistening sheen showing the full extent of his emotion.

"Zack." I put a hand on his cheek. "I know, really. I forgive you. Just, no more lying to my face, okay?"

"Okay."

He comes around to open the door for me like the gentleman he is. The unspoken questions I have about the proposal, the ring that's been sitting on my bedside table at Zoe's since we got back from Texas, the divorce he's kept a secret for over a year, all slide to the wayside as my fingers interlock with his.

There are more important things to talk about over juicy burgers and fries. Things like the Seattle mob and the strange man in my apartment. Because mob means bad guy. Text-book bad guy who has probably killed people... and that means Zoe is feeling a certain kind of way.

A kind of way that scares me.

Zack lets go of my hand to open the door. We step in, are seated at a window-side table with a candle between us, and are left to peruse the menu even though we both already know what we want to order.

This place was one of the first we went to together. Back when Zack suspected me of murdering ex-boyfriends.

I check my phone. No buzz from Zoe–yet. I have a feeling I'll get a slew of texts complaining about babysitting Nick.

"Zoe let me in," Zack says after folding his menu closed and setting it at the edge of the table.

I nod, still looking over the cocktails. "She sure did."

"And agreed to keep an eye on Nick."

"Yep."

"I was surprised."

I smile. "She likes you, Zack."

"She's your best friend. I figured she'd be more pissed at me than you are."

My mouth goes dry, the fear that he will realize just how angry she's gotten about men in my past flashing through my head. Not for the first time, I wonder what would happen if he ever found out? If he ever dusted off the solved cases and took a closer look now that he knows her so much better.

I shake out of my spiraling thoughts and smirk at him. "Well, you're the best guy I've ever dated by a *mile*, so I think she's on board with keeping you around."

And not killing you, I add silently. Not that Zoe is killing anyone right now. She promised.

"Speaking of friends willing to go to bat..." I raise an eyebrow.

The waitress hustles up, and I put my question aside. We order, my stomach already rumbling at the promise of seasoned garlic fries, then I return my focus to my boyfriend.

"What's the deal with Nick? What did he do to earn lie-to-your-girlfriend-and-fly-across-the-country loyalty?"

Zack frowns, concern flashing across his face for a second before he spots my smile and relaxes a bit.

He settles into his chair, a habit from when he records for the podcast. "I was living in Seattle for a while, just a few years to get a change of scenery and try to figure out the course of my life. I didn't have the podcast yet."

I nod, thanking the waitress as she sets down my raspberry cocktail. It sounded delicious a minute ago, but the blood-red color of the drink has me re-thinking my order. "That case was the first one, right?"

"Yeah. Nick is a big reason Armchair Detective even started." He looks down, picking at his napkin. "I didn't know anyone, but I knew I wanted to get into journalism."

"You did a year at the University of Washington."

"I did. Well, more like a semester. Then one night I was in the wrong place at the wrong time."

I raise an eyebrow, spinning my glass on the tablecloth.

Zack continues, "I'd gone to the corner store for some stuff, and it got robbed. The guy who did it was some politician's son—so the cops took me in for it instead."

Disgust splashes into my stomach. My lip curls. "What?"

"Yeah. I thought it was so I could give my statement or whatever." He grimaces. "But then they started fingerprinting me."

"Yeesh. Zack..."

He shakes his head. "It was gonna be bad, Kar. But it turned out I wasn't the only one in the store."

"Nick?"

He huffs out a grin. "He was back by the ice cream and saw the whole thing. Watched the actual asshole who stuck up the place get cornered by the cops a block down. Watched them take his gun and put him in a squad car.

But he knew something I didn't. He knew who the guy was, and he knew those cops."

"How did he get you out of it?"

Zack leans into the table, blowing out a breath through pursed lips. "Like I said, he knew the cops. Followed us to the station, and when they started fingerprinting me, he said some stuff that changed their attitude real fast."

"They just let you go?" I sip my drink, fury at the injustice he's gone through heating my veins.

"Not much they could do when he threatened to expose their ties to his," Zack does finger quotes, "*organization*." He grins again. "Pretty sure he got in some trouble with his uncle for doing that."

"The uncle that's in prison."

Zack shakes his head. "This was before all that. Nick got me out of a false arrest I would've had no way of fighting. We were in the cop shop almost all night while they argued. And then I bought him breakfast, we got to talking, and the beginnings of Armchair Detective were born."

I nod slowly, connecting dots to paint a picture of Zack all those years ago. A different man than the one I know, but one with all the tenacity and craving for truth that I recognize today. Characteristics he shares with Zoe. Ones that made me fall in love with him.

"You wanted to take those cops down."

"I did. And so did Nick. He never liked the family working with law enforcement. Well, never liked them working with *anyone* they had to bribe."

My mind flashes to a blade in my hand, metal slicing through flesh to stop a deranged lunatic from killing my best friend and the man I was falling in love with. A memory that usually brings nausea to my throat and frantic writing in my journal to get past. But this time I feel a flutter of pride.

After a moment of silence, I murmur, "True loyalty isn't paid for."

Zack catches my eye. "That's what Nick earned from me that day. And every day after as we got to know each other. He helped me write the story that got those cops suspended."

I roll my eyes at the light punishment.

He shrugs a shoulder. "It was enough to convince the Farelli family to stop working with them. And the money from the paper gave me the funds for my equipment."

"And then you brought down Nick's uncle?"

Zack sighs. "That was another year later. And it nearly broke Nick to do it. He believed in that man. Frank was like a father to him, but he broke a cardinal rule of the family."

"Did you ask for Nick's help? Or did Nick come to you to make the case?"

Another sigh, heavier this time. "It was mutual. I'd gotten some contacts with the feds at that point, from my various digging for occasional stories for the paper. One of my guys told me about some really bad shit going on. I called Nick just after he found out the same. We..." He runs a hand across his face, staring out across the steadily filling dining room. "We took Frank down. He's serving a life sentence now."

"Damn," I murmur. The waitress returns, carefully setting down plates and warning us that they're hot. I pluck a fry from mine, smother it in ketchup, and plop it into my mouth.

Very hot. But delicious. Even my stomach, still churning a bit with retroactive anger for Zack, is pleased by the presence of food.

"Okay," I say after chewing and swallowing.

Zack raises an eyebrow as the waitress scurries away. "Okay?"

"Okay," I repeat. "I get it. I'm officially not mad about you ditching out on the trip and rescuing Nick from Seattle. I get it. In fact, let me shoot Zoe a text to make sure everything is going well over there."

He stifles a grin. "Thanks."

I type away on my phone while Zack digs into his food. My mind wanders across the details of his story. Alone in a new city, trying to build a business from the ground up... newly divorced.

He left that part out of the story, but I'm almost entirely certain that's the reason he left Spokane in the first place. His ex is alive and well, living her best life on the east coast with a husband and two kids—thanks for the information, Zoe.

Zack married her in a hurry. And, granted, they were very young… but why do *I* require this much time to think about it?

"Uh…"

I blink up at Zack. My eyes are dry. I've been spacing into the distance while he eats. My fries are going cold.

"Sorry." I snap back to the present, frustrated by my own fixation on a thing I can't control. Is this how Zoe feels when she's presented with a problem she can't solve? That would certainly explain the copious amounts of spacing out she does.

"Your food okay?"

I shrug. "It's great, as usual." I bristle a bit. Surely he knows why I'm not all here tonight. We've solved what I deem to be the more important of the two issues between us. But that elephant is still there… waiting.

I sink my teeth into the burger. Zack watches me, his dark eyes hooded with something like caution.

"Kar, I wanted to…"

I hesitate mid-chew, then set the burger down and swallow. "What?"

"About Christmas and what you asked."

I purse my lips, trying to keep a neutral expression as he dances around the subject we've been so valiantly avoiding. "Yes?"

He opens his mouth.

My phone vibrates.

I feel an eye twitch coming on. A quick glance shows Zoe's unnervingly beautiful smile glinting up from the screen. Shit.

"Hold that thought," I say with something of a regretful groan in my voice. Worry laces through me. Along with the low hum of regret that whatever Zack was about to say is possibly gone—for the evening, at least. I snatch up the phone and answer with a brusque, "Why are you calling me?"

Something is wrong. Absolutely has to be for her to interrupt tonight. My mind conjures up images of Nick, dead in an alley and Zoe standing over him with a knife. Or, worse, cops putting pieces of already 'solved' murders together and pushing her into the back of a squad car.

Zoe responds in a terse whisper. "I went to hang with the Cannoli or whatever, but he was leaving right when I got there."

My eyes go wide. Zack raises a brow. I wave my hand in a 'wrap up' gesture and he immediately goes to flag down the waitress.

"Oh, God, Zoe. Why are you whispering?" I demand, my voice mimicking hers without me meaning to.

"I followed him."

I'm already out of my seat and pulling my jacket from the back of my chair. Zack gives up on the check. He tosses cash onto the table, more than enough to cover our meal and tip. Without a question or hesitation, he hurries ahead of me, pulling the door open and matching my speed as we rush to the car.

A TALE OF TWO KNIVES

I follow the Cannoli to a more kitschy part of town, one that harkens back to the small clustered neighborhoods of the east coast with local bodegas and family-owned, hole-in-the-wall businesses.

They're boxy brick buildings linked together like a little family holding hands along the street. Most are closed this time of night, but the one the Cannoli parks in front of still has lights on, though it's clearly after hours. It's a butcher shop I've never heard of, though that's unsurprising. Frankly, this part of town isn't one I'd make a point of spending time in, let alone driving through.

I'm far enough behind him that I flip my lights off and pull over in a dark part of the street, hoping I've gone unnoticed. The engine is quiet, but I leave it running in case this isn't his final destination. Being that he's from Seattle, he could very well be checking the map for where he really needs to go.

That hypothesis is quickly dashed when the Cannoli gets out of the car. He glances both ways while walking around the hood to the butcher shop—watchful, but he doesn't seem overly concerned. He's used to being untouchable, and it's doubtful anyone knows he's in Spokane. He probably never considered that TCT would ask me to check in on him, or that I would follow him if he went anywhere.

To be fair, TCT probably never considered the possibility that the Cannoli would go anywhere, either.

My phone buzzes in my pocket. I know it's a text from Karrie before looking. Best friend ESP aside, she's really the only person who'd text me. My father can't figure it out and my mother refuses. Tom would send any messages through Karrie.

How's it going with Nick?

Either one or both of them is avoiding the hard conversation they need to have, which elicits a sly smile from me, despite the fact that I'm alone.

I type back: *He's alive.*

Ha, she responds, though I know she doesn't think that's funny, given my history.

Debating for a minute as I watch the Cannoli cut between the butcher shop and the building next to it, I decide not to elaborate on my answer to Karrie's question.

Adding a "for now" would incite a panic that might be entirely unnecessary. Maybe the guy likes fresh cuts of meat. Can't say I blame him, knowing how the food industry handles such things. This place doesn't inspire much confidence, though. And considering the hour...

Still, doubt niggles its way in, and I just can't trust whatever is happening out of my sight. Leaning across my center console, I pop the glove box open and palm one of the smaller knives I've invested in over the years. I've never actually killed with it, but it's an excellent size for just-in-case scenarios. Not that I'm ever a slap-dash murderer, but ya know. It could cut a decent steak if the occasion called for it.

After slipping out of my car with slow, precise movements, I pop onto the sidewalk and jog along the shadows, picturing my night stalking Mac and channeling my inner feline hunter.

Something about this situation feels a little precarious, so I decide to call Karrie just in case it goes south and this meat butcher is a front for another kind of butcher. I might be a bit overconfident in myself, but I'm not stupid.

She doesn't say hello, probably already figuring something is up. "Why are you calling me?" Based on the tightness of her words, she definitely knows things aren't copacetic.

I glance around and curve my hand over my mouth. "I went to hang with the Cannoli or whatever, but he was leaving right when I got there."

"Oh, God, Zoe. Why are you whispering?" Her voice drops a level in volume to match mine, the anxiety winding tighter.

"I followed him." *Duh.* "He drove to this rundown part of town and went into an alley behind this sketch-ass butcher shop. Might be a '*butcher shop*' knowing the Cannoli, if you know what I mean."

She gasps, and I hear her relaying what I'm saying to Tom. "Zoe, do not go to the sketch-ass butcher shop. Stay in the car."

I creep along the wall and peek around the corner. Light from an open door spills in a bright chunk onto the asphalt and illuminates Nick's feet and legs. He's face-to-face with a shorter man whose apron is filthy with red and brown stains. I'm not going to bother speculating if it's just animal blood. The man appears to be frozen in place.

"Zoe, what's happening?"

I don't answer, almost like I've been frozen, too. The fragility of the moment is evident in the charged stare-down happening a few yards away from me.

It all shatters when the guy speaks, his trance broken as the Cannoli's appearance fully settles in.

"Oh shit," he spits, scrambling backwards. It's a comically cartoonish move that's halted when the Cannoli snatches him by the back of his shirt and yanks him out, flipping him and slamming his back into the brick wall.

"Zoe!"

I flinch and turn down the volume on my phone. "Hush," I whisper, straining to hear what might happen next.

The Cannoli's face is half-illuminated by the light still falling out of the back door, but his expression is unreadable. It's impressively terrifying, though from where I stand, I just find it incredibly interesting. From the shorter man's view, it'd be sufficiently intimidated.

The guy sputters, fingers scrabbling against the Cannoli's fists wrapped around the front of his shirt. "I did what I was told. I disappeared. I didn't say a damn thing."

The Cannoli's head cocks to the side, the move oddly robotic because the question I read in the movement doesn't register in his face.

"You turned state's evidence," the Cannoli growls.

So it's a guy on the Farelli family's hit list. The Cannoli must've known WITSEC placed him here. Spokane was historically a popular WITSEC relocation destination.

The guy's ragged breaths are all that fill the silence that follows the Cannoli's words, and I'm on fire with curiosity for how this plays out.

"N-no," the guy says. "They took out my boy and told me to get lost if I wanted to keep the rest of my family alive."

"We don't do kids," the Cannoli says, not so much defensive as confused.

"*Frank* didn't do kids," the butcher clarifies. "Things are different now."

The Cannoli's grip on the guy loosens as those words settle in his mind. "Someone took out your kid." It's not a question, though confusion envelopes his posture, if not his expression. The way he speaks, it's like he's running through details in his mind.

It makes me wish he was a computer I could hack. I want to scroll through those thoughts, make notes, dig deep.

"Officially listed as an accident. But you know the difference between a real accident and a rigged one. I'm not stupid, either." The butcher is rubbing at his chest, but he's sounding more confident now that the Cannoli doesn't have him in a death grip.

"Who?" the Cannoli demands.

The butcher sends him a glare that has my estimation of his chutzpah at an all-time high. "I got out of that mess. If you don't know, you're on your own."

"Give me something," the Cannoli says this through his teeth. "Carlotta?"

"You figure it out, and don't come back here. Just you being here puts what's left of my family in danger."

Karrie says my name again, reminding me that the phone is in my hand. I'd pulled it away from my ear so I could hear better. And now my mind is spinning with possibilities, fingers itching to start doing research on this butcher guy's son.

"Um," I say distractedly, spinning to press my back against the wall around the corner from the Cannoli and the butcher, trying to get my bearings.

Carlotta (aka Prima Donna—hello, Phantom of the Opera!) is his much older cousin who took over the family business after her father went down for child trafficking five years before. It's some sort of moral line they toed. Some mobsters have certain standards, apparently, and this is one the Cannoli held close. Prima Donna's on my list. But so is Frank (aka the Saint because obviously we love irony), her dad and the Cannoli's uncle who's in prison. He could've ordered the hit easily from behind bars. Then there's Georgie (aka Neck because that tree trunk is all you see in photos), another of the Cannoli's uncles, who maybe held a grudge for the part the Cannoli played in getting Frank the Saint locked up. The possibilities continue to spin in my mind, and I'm almost as frustrated as the Cannoli that this butcher isn't giving the information up.

"Where are you?" Karrie sounds breathless, like she's moving. "We'll meet you there."

I tsk and shake my head. "I'm sending my location," I whisper. "I think the Cannoli just got some upsetting news."

The conversation in the back alley seems to have wrapped up, and I send a quick location pin to Karrie. I trap my breath in my lungs and pull my knife from my pocket, gripping my phone like it's my second weapon. I don't like how little noise comes from around the corner.

Do I dare check the scene? For all I know, they've simply gone inside.

I've just taken my first fresh toke of oxygen, leaning to peek around the corner, when a gut feeling has every muscle in my body seizing.

You expect metal to be cold against your skin, especially this time of year, this time of night. But I suspect the Cannoli's had his own blade stowed in a pocket, imbued with the warmth of his body heat so that the nip at my throat is less startling.

It's my instincts that saved me from walking into that knife, though the cold would have been a better warning.

"Zoe!" Karrie shouts in my ear.

The Cannoli's eyes flicker to the phone and back to my eyes.

"What are you doing here?" His voice is strangely calm, almost uninterested.

Fascinating.

I hang up on Karrie, using as little movement as possible. I don't lower my phone hand, cautious, though I strangely don't feel afraid. A warm sense of one-upmanship floods me, and I want to knock this cocky mobster down a peg.

"Tom asked me to check on you."

One of his eyes narrows, though the corner of his mouth lifts slightly. "So you followed me here? That's not smart. I could easily kill you."

That competitive nature rears its head again, and I raise a brow. I use the knife in my own hand, which I hadn't had time to bring up in my original self-defense position, to tap against a very tender part on his lower body. It might not be my first choice, but it turns out to be a much more effective move than I anticipated.

Like most men, he flinches noticeably at the slightest threat to his manhood. The caveman flash of panic in his eyes is deliciously satisfying. I almost grin.

"Funny," I say, a little smug. "So could I."

WHO WANTS TO KILL NICK?

"Shit, shit, shit, shit." I can't stop the repetitive mantra-like muttering as Zack roars the car down dingy back alleys, following Google's instructions and turning left. My emotions are on a roller coaster, switching so fast between fear for my best friend and fury over her hanging up on me that I'm about to get whiplash.

"Almost there," Zack says through clenched teeth. Stress radiates off him in waves.

He trusts Nick. But how much? Enough to have Zoe babysit the man, but he doesn't know what she is really capable of. And do either of us know what Nick is capable of?

"Don't go there," I murmur to myself.

Zack doesn't glance at me; his gaze is solidly fixed on the road ahead. But he says, "He won't hurt her."

"That's not what I'm worried about," I say, biting back the rest of my response because he doesn't need to know that my concern is finding Nick in a pool of blood, not Zoe.

We swing around a final turn and the headlights fall on two figures standing at the open end of an alley. Zoe, almost as tall as the mobster, doesn't even look at us. But Nick's head whips around, the blade he had to my friend's throat falling to his side.

It takes a few seconds for Zoe to do the same, though her knife was considerably lower.

I open the door with Zack following suit. He leaves the car running. The headlights cast an eerie yellow glow on the cracked and stained brick buildings. Nick, at least, has the grace to look like he was caught doing something stupid.

Zoe appears completely unfazed.

"What." I move forward, pulling my coat tighter around me as I inch over a patch of ice. "The." Nick takes half a step back. "Fuck."

Zack swallows. "Guys, why do you both have knives out?"

My stomach does a little flip, and I aim my glare at Zoe. "Excellent question, babe. To go along with a litany of other questions I have. Like, *what the fuck?*"

A single flake of snow drifts down, glistening in the light before it hits asphalt.

Despite my heaving, frustrated breaths, I swallow down the anger, inhaling a deep breath through pursed lips and unclenching my jaw. "Everyone go back to the apartment. Now. We will discuss this in the warm living room." My lip curls. "*Without* blades."

It's a mark of how pissed I must look, because I get zero kick back from the mobster or the serial killer. Zoe tucks the little blade into her jacket pocket and nods. Nick slips his into a sheath at his side. He gives Zack a long stare, then dips his head and strides down the quickly dampening street to the rental car parked a block away.

I rub the bridge of my nose and walk to the car. "Home."

Zack climbs into the driver's seat. True to form as an amazing boyfriend—if not one capable of answering a simple question—he turns up the heater and plugs in his phone to blast some Enya.

"I just..." I scowl out the windshield. The snow is falling faster now, bringing a gust of white that obscures some of the way ahead. "What were they thinking?" I demand.

Zack flicks a glance my way. "What do you mean?"

"Fucking knives out in the middle of the street?" I practically spit the words, knowing I need to cool off some of this temper before we get home. "Idiotic, Zack. It was idiotic. Not something *either* of them are. So what the fuck?"

He doesn't respond. Which is fair since it was a rhetorical question.

A few minutes pass with thudding bass and stunning vocals. I stare out the window, mind swirling with the possibilities of what could have happened tonight.

Zack reaches over and turns the music down as we get closer to home. He scratches his forehead, brow furrowed. Something is rolling around inside his head. Charging up to become words.

Finally, he says, "I get Nick."

I stretch my neck, heat and frustration causing knots. "Get him about what?"

Zack shakes his head. "I'm looking forward to his explanation for why he left the safety of the apartment, but I get him having a blade. Why the hell does Zoe have one?"

A chill sends goosebumps along my arms. I swallow, even angrier now that I have to address this. All because Zoe couldn't keep it in her pants—the knife, that is. She didn't *have* to follow a mafia enforcer into a sketchy alley. You'd think a decade of stalking and murder would have given her a little more patience.

"Protection, probably," I murmur. Not a lie. Not really. Then I reach across and turn the music back up.

I almost expect him to shut it off. To ask me more questions and probe into the reasoning behind Zoe wielding a knife like Gordon-fucking-Ramsey. Instead, he makes an abrupt right turn that extends the length of our drive a bit.

I realize why as he pulls into a parking place at my favorite cookie shop.

"Be right back," he says as he hops out and rushes through the snow.

Two minutes later, he returns with a pale blue box tied with a ribbon. He doesn't say a word. Just gets back in and takes us the rest of the way home.

By the time we pull into the parking lot, some of my anger has subsided. Some. Not all.

Zoe has a key to the apartment. Even if I hadn't given her one, she'd have snuck mine and made a copy. So finding her and Nick both waiting outside in the hallway mollifies my mood even more.

I unlock the door without a word, stride into my home, and remove my shoes and coat. The others do the same, and Zack disappears into the kitchen for a moment while we all get settled.

While the other two get settled. I can't sit. My heart pounds with the residual frustration coursing through my veins. I pace, stalking up the living room and back. Zoe sits on one end of the couch, her legs crossed, back straight, arms folded over her lap as she watches me with those brilliant blue eyes.

I should tell her Zack asked about the knife. Or should I keep it to myself? What *would* her reaction be if he discovered our secret?

My insides twist at the thought of hiding another thing from another loved one. Looking for something to be mad at, I turn to Nick.

He seems to have gotten used to being here these last few days. He lounges, also watching me with wary eyes, but looks more comfortable in my home than Zoe does.

"Kar—"

I whip around, facing my friend and glaring daggers. "Yes, Zoe? My incredibly intelligent friend who definitely knows better than to pull a knife out in public? Did you have something to say?"

Zoe, for the first time in a long time, looks appropriately chagrined. "I'm sorry," she says, her voice low but clear.

Like a punctured balloon, the rest of my temper deflates. I close my eyes. She and I will have to discuss this further another time. When Zack isn't there, and I can properly explain the reason I'm so angry.

"There was no one around," Nick says. His gruff voice carries a hint of exasperation.

Zoe purses her lips and widens her eyes, leaning away from the new target of my glare.

"No?" I grimace. "Do you know that? Or are you guessing?"

He doesn't say anything.

"For all you know," I continue, "it could have been a cop coming around that corner."

Nick stretches, his unconcerned expression drawing a frown from Zoe. "Listen, Karrie—"

"No, you listen." I stride to him, leaning forward with my hands on my hips. "Caution. That's the takeaway here. Use some fucking caution. Someone tried to kill you, Nick. Someone thought you were in enough danger that they called Zack to come collect you. And then, while he was out rescuing you, you got *shot at!* So parading yourself around the sketch-ass part of town—" I catch Zoe's grin out of the corner of my eye "—is a dumb thing to do. Neither of you are dumb. Act like it."

Zoe fidgets. My gaze turns to her.

"Why were either of you pulling knives in the first place?" I ask with half a groan.

"I'd like to get an answer to that one, too," Zack declares as he pushes through the hall door. He's got the blue box in his hands, lid off, the smell of rich chocolate chip cookies filling the air.

I smile, take the cookie he offers me, and settle myself into the plump armchair in the corner, my job of scolding the murdery children accomplished.

"I didn't know it was her," Nick mutters, his low voice unsettling as he casts a look at Zoe.

"I knew it was him," Zoe says, unhelpfully. "But I recently found out some things, and he was being shady as shit. Why go to a random butcher's? Why threaten the man?"

The mobster doesn't speak. He runs a hand through his hair, shaggy still, but clean. I take a bite of my cookie, a spark of curiosity lighting up as he gives Zoe a split second glance that she doesn't notice.

"Nick." Zack sets the cookies on the coffee table and stares down at his friend. "I brought you here to help you, but that help is limited if you don't tell us what you know."

"That's part of the damn problem," Nick spits out. His hands are clenched before him, the nonchalant attitude about being in trouble replaced with frustration as Zack tugs on the bond between them. "I don't..."

"You don't know what you know," Zoe finishes.

I look from her to Nick, my brow furrowed. "What exactly does that mean? We've already established you don't know why your family is after you. Why go to the butcher's?"

"He's a cousin. Was part of the family for a long time, but right after my uncle got pinched, he disappeared. WITSEC is what everyone said. The whole family, up and gone." Nick shakes his head. "That never sat with me, though. He wouldn't have liked what my uncle was into any more than the rest of us, but Frank was in jail before he ran. So why go to the feds?"

"He didn't," Zoe answers. She meets my eye before looking at Nick. "That's what I overheard, at least. He left because he was scared. His kid was killed."

My stomach clenches.

Nick's face twists into a look of anger. "Yeah, which is why I need answers. Someone lied to me. Either him, or someone in the family. If it was someone back in Seattle–"

"Maybe that's who's after you now," I mutter. My cookie has a single bite taken out, the rest getting melty chocolate all over my hand.

"But that still doesn't answer why." Zack passes me a paper towel.

I take it, wiping the chocolate from my fingers and placing my cookie on it to avoid further mess. Nick wrinkles his nose.

I frown at him.

"Well, whoever is after you has already found one target," Zoe says, breaking the silence.

Nick's brow furrows.

She purses her lips. "I wasn't sure when to bring it up. But that guy," Zoe directs her gaze at Zack "the one who gave you the tip to get Nick outta there… he's dead."

Zack spits his sip of water.

"Stretch?" Nick almost whispers the word, his deep voice tinged with something that sounds like regret.

Zoe nods. "Cops labeled it as an accident, but given his warning and the whole mob thing…" She waves a hand through the air. "It's definitely a cover for a hit. Especially with the amount of blood."

A shudder runs down my spine.

"When?" I ask.

Zoe and I exchange a significant look. "He was found earlier today."

My mouth goes dry, and I turn wide eyes on Zack. "If you hadn't gotten out of Seattle when you did…"

Zack steps closer, putting out his hand for me to hold. I do, the strain between us nothing compared to the icy fear that comes with knowing he might not have made it out of Seattle alive.

"Again," Zack says after a few seconds of unsettled silence. "Why?"

"We won't know why until we do some digging," Zoe announces. She reaches down and pulls her laptop from her bag. "I've already made a codex of names we needed to look into."

With a pointed look at Nick that makes me raise my eyebrows, Zoe flips open her computer and starts typing with surprising ease for someone with long pink nails.

"There's Prima Donna. Carlotta," she adds when confusion overtakes all our expressions. "Obviously. She's the head of the organization, fingers in every pie. At least, that's her reputation. A lot less delegation than the old guard."

Nick's eyes go wide.

"Then Georgie the Neck, her second in command, but one of the older family members still running the main elements of business."

"He might have beef with me for a couple reasons," Nick says. He runs a hand across his face, eyes still wide as he adds to Zoe's copious amount of information. "He and my dad were rivals for half a second in the old days. It didn't last long."

"Hmm." Zoe chews her tongue thoughtfully. "Good to know." She uses her mouse pad for a second, then gets back to typing too fast.

I set my uneaten cookie on the table with a glance at Zack. He's the only one still standing. He isn't fazed by Zoe's sleuthing. It's not exactly new. But he and I do exchange another baffled look as our friends talk over names I've never heard.

I rise as Zoe asks Nick about the last name. Another uncle who was part of Frank's inner circle before shit went down.

What *shit* specifically happened has yet to be explained to me. But I know Zoe; we will get there. So, while those two list the reasons any of the three names might be after Nick, I scurry to the office and return a moment later with a fresh notebook, a stack of black and red gel pens, and a purple highlighter.

I plunk down on the floor, drawing Zoe from her conversation as she winces at me sitting on the ground. Then she arches an immaculate eyebrow.

"What are you doing?"

I grin up at her, uncapping my gel pen and scrawling *Who Wants to Kill Nick?* at the top of my paper. "Last time we did this, there were dead bodies all over the damn place.

This time I get to help solve the puzzle without having to throw up every couple of minutes!"

Behind me, Zack chuckles. He crosses and settles in next to Nick. "This is what I was saying, man. If anyone is gonna help us figure out this shit... it's these two."

Chapter Ten

SCOOBY INVASION

"We're going to Scooby with the gang tonight!" Karrie says brightly as soon as I answer my phone.

As if I wasn't "scoobying" on my own already. I have news to share, and I'm looking forward to the impressed and shocked faces it will garner. The last time I did my big reveal, the reaction I got gave me such a boost that I'm looking for a repeat.

The Cannoli called it. I do like to be the smartest person in the room.

Between work assignments today, I've been checking and rechecking the database for the autopsy report on Stretch—born Harold Alborghetti (if anyone deserves a nickname, it's this guy)—and finally struck gold. I wouldn't have been able to sit on this big news very long. I knew there would be something here, especially after I did some digging on the butcher's kid.

If this wasn't happening tonight, I would've called for a meeting. Or I would've showed up at their apartment with a food bribe.

"The plan is to be at your place in an hour," Karrie continues, oblivious to my silence. It's not unusual.

I wrinkle my nose, looking at all my pristine surfaces. Though I regularly miss having Karrie here, not having to worry about her myriad dates contaminating my home has made me settle further into my germophobic ways. The idea of allowing it to happen now makes my skin prickle.

"My place?" I ask darkly.

"Yeah, Zack just got a shipment of stuff that's taking over the living room, so we don't have enough space for everyone."

I can *feel* the whine enter my voice before the words even come out. "But Karrie—"

"We're going to get pad Thai for dinner—our treat," she says in a singsong voice. "And I bought extra wipes. The kind you like."

Damn it. Pad Thai does sound good. "Fine."

She squeals, which I'm unprepared for—usually I know to pull the phone away from my ear. This time, it happens belatedly, and I have to switch sides so I can rub at my ear drum.

"This has been so fun!" she continues.

"That's because it doesn't involve dead bodies," I point out.

She makes a soft gagging sound that is entirely put-on. Her real gag sounds like a cat about to ralph.

They arrive a little over an hour later, which has been the case since they've had the cannoli staying with them. I wonder what it is he does that delays them because Karrie might seem flighty, but she's the most punctual person I've ever known. I have no idea about Tom's timeliness, but with Karrie, it doesn't matter. They're always on time together.

The Cannoli keeps his hands in his pockets as they walk in, and he surveys my apartment with a mountain lion's casual attentiveness. Like a predator looking for its prey's means of escape. He takes his shoes off and sets them on the rack before anyone even shows him that's protocol, and the move is so fluid, I know it's rote.

Karrie sighs as she watches, her lips pursed, and I note how red his hands look. Like he's washed them a number of times recently. That would explain Karrie's mild irritation.

"I thought you were bringing dinner," I say by way of greeting.

"We ordered, but it's not ready yet," TCT says just as his phone beeps out an alert. "Oh! There it is. Babe, want to come with?"

Karrie shoots me a pleading look, so I shrug to let her know it's fine. I wonder if having the Cannoli in their personal space is wearing on her. Maybe she's planning to bug him about his answer to the proposal. Or maybe she's looking to get a car quickie in. I don't know.

She grins and floats out the door, her hand sliding into Tom's.

I turn to the Cannoli, who stands just inside the living room, his expression mild.

Mac meows and graces us with his presence, which surprises me since he's almost as avoidant of new people as I am. Karrie, he knows, of course. And my parents bribed him with treats.

Unfortunately, he's never warmed much to TCT, though he doesn't snub him entirely.

But Mac goes right up to the Cannoli like he's an actual cannoli and rubs against his leg like some sort of extroverted golden retriever.

The Cannoli doesn't stoop to stroke the soft fur. "Cats are notorious carriers of disease. Their litter boxes alone..." He gives a violent shudder.

"I trained him to use the toilet," I reply. "And he stays indoors. Mostly." I cast a chastising gaze in Mac's direction.

The Cannoli grunts in response, but I can tell he's considering.

"Make yourself comfortable." I gesture toward the couch. "I just steam cleaned it yesterday."

He shoots me an appreciative look as he moves in that direction. When he settles into the couch, Mac jumps onto the coffee table and stares at him expectantly.

The Cannoli doesn't move. "What's its name?"

Mac hops to my desk to perch himself closer.

"Machete. Mac for short."

The Cannoli lifts a brow at me before finally complying and stroking Mac's head, and, surprise of all surprises, smiles in response when the cat's motor kicks on. His purrs are louder than the motorcycle that belongs to the guy two doors down.

The silence is so unexpectedly *comfortable* that I want to crawl out of my own skin. So I go to the kitchen to get us a couple glasses of wine and come back to the living room to find Mac in the Cannoli's lap while he leans over my desk. He's got a pocket pouch of sanitary wipes and smooths it down the surfaces he can reach without disturbing my cat.

I find it inexplicably rage-inducing.

I offer the glass of wine to him and sip my own, thinking it's probably not the best idea on an empty stomach, but I can't help tossing a large gulp back.

"I recognized the blade you had," the Cannoli says without looking at me. He holds his wineglass in one hand while petting Mac with the other.

It's the first time he's mentioned the knife situation at all. We've sort of carried on since Karrie's scolding as if it hadn't happened. TCT hasn't asked about why I had a knife, or why Karrie reacted the way she did, not since that night, anyway. I assume she gave him a decent enough explanation. My bombshell reveal certainly distracted him enough from asking more about it at the time.

She pulled me aside to give me a private upbraiding about using more caution, revealing her true reason for being so upset: she's paranoid about me getting arrested and all of my crimes suddenly coming to light, despite our successful framing of her ex-stalker.

It's sweet that she would worry so much. But it's not like I had a machete or something, and it's doubtful law enforcement would do much if I took out a known mafia player, even if self-defense was a dubious label. In this case, it would've been believable.

"Spyderco makes a good knife," I finally respond.

The Cannoli leans back, swirling his wine in the glass and eyeing me with that mild disinterest I have come to recognize. His expression betrays little, as usual. "So what's your story?"

It's posed casually, but that question spikes my irritation as I stare at his neutral, objectively handsome face.

"My story," I repeat dryly.

One side of his mouth quirks up. "You don't buy a knife like that and use it the way you did and not have a story behind it."

"I have a thing for blades."

His smile grows larger, and my eyes narrow further. "Yes, but why?"

I wait a beat. "They're quiet."

He tips his head, regarding me like I'm a cute puppy doing tricks. "They also require very close proximity."

I say nothing, my gaze unwavering as I tip my wineglass to my lips.

"Also messy," he continues. His eyes do a sweep from my head to my toes, but the look lacks the usual lasciviousness I've dealt with since puberty. It's well and truly an academic perusal. "That doesn't seem like it'd be your style."

"And what's your style? Strangulation?"

The slightest pinch comes into his expression, and a little thrill of victory shoots through me. I like knowing something about him that he wasn't expecting. I like feeling like I'm the one with the upper hand.

"I believe strangulation is messy at times, too, isn't it? Victims tend to... void as they expire."

He doesn't move, but he grips his wineglass tighter. "There are methods to avoid this."

"Hm." I tap a finger against my glass and move across the room to my desk with the weight of his attention on me. I ignore it, though, feeling pretty good about myself right about now.

He watches me log back into my laptop and pull up the browser.

"Shouldn't you wait for the other two members of your weird investigative unit?"

"They'll be here in a few minutes," I reply without looking up. "My app alerted me that Karrie was within a mile radius."

His focus on me grows heavier along my skin. "You two are close."

It's not a question, and it irritates me. Just another thing on a growing list. "I don't think that could be any more obvious."

"She the one you kill for?" His words drop into the air like baseball-sized rocks into a pond.

It's odd to have someone, outside of Karrie, know this fact about me and say it so casually. Of course he would be nonchalant about it. His kill list is likely longer than mine. I turn in my chair to meet his gaze.

"Zack doesn't know," he continues. "He probably would've mentioned it."

Probably would've turned me in, I add silently, but I don't say it. Something about the look on the Cannoli's face makes me think for a moment that I said it out loud. I know I didn't. I have amazing self-control.

"I won't say anything," the Cannoli adds with a smile.

I squint at him. "Should I thank you for that?"

He lifts one shoulder, still smiling.

What a prick. I'm not sure why *that* irks me. But it does. I turn back to my laptop.

"So you kill for your friend. And you also help her boyfriend solve cases for his show."

One slow inhale keeps me from snapping at him. My voice is calm when I respond: "We helped one other time. I just happen to be good at research, and Tom is set on helping you. Karrie joined because she loves him. I joined because I love her."

"That was the case about all her dead ex-boyfriends."

He's getting me back. His revenge for me knowing more than he wants me to is showing me that he knows more than I want him to. I give him a flat look. He's never taken his gaze from me, and I'm considering changing his nickname to Stares A Lot.

"You don't have to play dumb with me," Stares A Lot says, laughing. "I actually admire your devotion to your friend and the clever way you covered your tracks. Being an enforcer for a crime family means I have to get creative about keeping my name off the suspect list."

"I didn't frame an innocent man, if that's what you're implying." Indignation edges my tone.

He raises his hands in surrender but says nothing.

"He deserved to go down for what he did. He would've killed TCT if we hadn't done something about it."

"Doesn't hurt that all your dirty deeds got buried with him," Stares A Lot—SAL—says, but it's admiration in his voice now. "Truly genius."

I feel like this genuine compliment shouldn't make a warmth spread through my chest like I just received some kind of academic excellence award. This guy is a legit murderer, more cold-hearted than me—I don't think he has many compunctions about who he kills, aside from the kid thing—so it's like praise from one professional to another.

My mother, the therapist, would probably have some shrinky words to say about my reaction to the flattery.

We've established that I'm a sociopath, though, right? Self-diagnosed, of course. From a young age, I've been aware enough to hide this little side of myself from my mother, who, admittedly, keeps some blinders on about the dysfunction that goes on in her own family.

I purse my lips as I do a search through local posts about the general area SAL frequented. I want to save my big reveal for when the others get back, but I need to keep my mind occupied so I don't dwell on the fact that my cat likes this guy and I feel comfortable, though deeply unsettled, about him being in my space.

"Did something happen out of the ordinary that led to Stretch thinking you might be in danger?" I ask.

He shrugs again. "Same old, same old as far as I know."

"Bribing cops, dumping bodies in the river, causing general fear and mayhem."

Out of the corner of my eye, I catch his smirk as he brings his wineglass to his lips again. Still staring at me. "I don't bribe cops."

I've done enough research to know his family runs a specific part of town, and I catch his chiseled profile on more than one security camera among the local businesses as I skip through cyberspace in a less-than-legal capacity.

Very little of it seems helpful. Grocery shopping, getting a sandwich from the same deli, and getting a new pair of shoes doesn't stand out as overly worrisome.

Then one shot catches my eye, and I pause the video, freezing SAL in the act of exiting a dark sedan. The unmistakable details around the image alert me to the fact that it's a prison.

Because I have a jumping-off point, I do a quick search on prisons near Seattle and double-back to the case that shook up his family's entire organization to find a perfect match to a Google maps comparison.

The front door opens just as I spin in my seat to settle a glare on SAL. "Nothing out of the ordinary, huh? Want to explain why you went to visit your uncle in prison two days before Stretch's warning?"

"Um, what?" Karrie says at the same time TCT shouts, "Nick!"

"Oh goody, everyone's here," I say, definitely not hiding the glee that's lighting a little fire in my belly.

SAL looks like Machete does when I catch him knocking stuff off my desk.

That fire grows. "What did your uncle tell you that might make someone nervous?"

SAL nudges Mac off of his lap and sets his wineglass aside. His forehead wrinkles and his lips form a tight, colorless line as he stands up to walk toward the window.

His troubled expression steals some of my smugness, and I'm disappointed I didn't one-up him and knock him down a peg. I legitimately switched him into worry mode.

"I never talked to him," he says softly, the gravel thicker at such a low volume.

"What do you mean?" TCT ushers Karrie further inside so they can set the take-out on the table.

SAL turns, his eyes following their movements, but his gaze is far away. "I went in, but I couldn't bring myself to see him. Frank practically raised me as his own. My dad was a deadbeat and an idiot, always getting thrown in jail for petty shit. He couldn't be trusted with very much. But Frank saw something in me and took me under his wing."

Karrie moves around behind SAL, her eyes the size of saucers as she catches my gaze. She mouths *Oh my God!* But I just shake my head at her.

"So when he was arrested for the trafficking—something he swore he'd never do—I was pissed." He runs a hand over his chin, and a spark of sympathy flares in my chest. Even Mac seems to sense SAL's distress and rubs against his legs. Irritation snuffs out my sympathy for the briefest of moments.

"I felt betrayed," SAL continues. "He'd lied to me all those years, pretending to be something he wasn't. We might have a very loose moral compass, but we believe in a code. That's non-negotiable."

Silence falls as we absorb this information. I'm mulling this over, turning it around and around in my mind, even as he continues.

"So why'd you go?" I wonder aloud, realizing when everyone looks at me that this might not be the right question.

"The anniversary of your dad's death," Karrie says softly. "December 19th."

We all turn to look at her. My shock is palpable.

"Yes, I do research, too," she says, disgruntled.

"I haven't seen him since he was arrested five years ago. But I felt like maybe I should…" SAL shrugs, at a loss. "I just couldn't do it.

There is something important about this aborted visit, something he hasn't seen yet, but I've got it pinned down.

I stand up, excited now, tossing the anniversary bit aside as irrelevant.

"You didn't go talk to him," I say, walking forward. "But someone thinks you did, and now they're worried."

SAL stops moving, his expression tightening as I approach. Gone are the worry lines, the soft vulnerability in his gaze disintegrating. He's locking onto my wave length, an intensity in his eyes.

"I think Frank the Saint knows something they don't want getting out."

SAL pulls in a long, deep breath, his eyes searching mine like he can read my thoughts there. "You want me to talk to him, don't you?"

I don't answer.

TCT clears his throat, and I realize SAL and I were staring at each other.

"We won't know what he knows until you do," I finally say, taking a step back and gesturing to the room at large. "It's not like any of us can call him up."

Chapter Eleven

MORE THAN A FEELING

S ushi and Zoe.

My heart is happy. Well, mostly happy. There's still that nagging question about *why the hell I haven't gotten an answer to my proposal yet.*

But we aren't thinking about that right now.

I clutch the thick brown paper bag to my chest. Warmth spreads through my fingers, the scent of tempura oozing through the folded and stapled top of the bag and causing my stomach to let out a dog-like growl as I walk up to Zoe's door. I don't knock; instead, I use my key and make sure to slip my shoes off first thing.

Zoe hasn't changed much about the apartment since I moved in with Zack. The shoe-rack is still placed strategically beside the door. Our friendship bracelet memento is hung above it, worn from the multitude of times we've given it a quick bop on the way in or out of the door. Her desk sits against the far wall, screen illuminated as she hunches over the keyboard (the only time she doesn't have immaculate posture is when she's researching).

"Kar?"

I chuckle as her curious greeting is drowned out by mewing from Machete. The little white fluffball likes me just fine, but I'm pretty sure the extra love on my shins is because he can smell the smoked salmon in my favorite sushi roll.

"Heyya, gorgeous," I say with a grin. I hoist the bag and carefully step around the cat toward Zoe. "It's girl's night."

Her soft huff of breath would be interpreted as an annoyed sigh by anyone else, but I catch the twitch of her lip and the glint in her eye. She likes this sushi place as much as I do. And our last few girl's nights were somewhat tinged with the whole *boyfriend lied to me* thing.

Tonight is going to be different. We are going to eat sushi, watch a movie, and discuss the case. Specifically… we are going to discuss Nick.

"When was this plan made?" Zoe rotates her chair back around, hand drifting to the mouse as she locks onto her computer screen.

"I made it. Today. The guys are going over what Nick might want to say on a phone call with Frank. It was getting tense. Well," I roll my eyes, "More tense. He's been an irritable mess since I called him out on the whole anniversary of his dad's death thing."

"Hmm."

"Zo," I say with a motherly tone. "Are you listening?"

"I'm trying to," she mutters, irritation flitting through her tone. "But I think I found something."

I drop the bag of sushi off on the kitchen ledge and hurry over to her side. "Lemme see."

"Wait."

"Hurmph," I grunt. I turn away from the screen where a pair of bodies on those metal slabs coroners use are displayed side-by-side. My stomach rolls, the familiar metallic taste of pre-vomit saliva coats my tongue.

I breathe in through my nose, exhaling through lips so pursed it almost becomes a whistle. I swallow a few times and wish I'd brought my journal. For whatever reason, writing about bodies is a helluva lot easier for me than looking at them.

"You okay?"

I nod, still not facing her computer. "Why, might I ask, do you have dead bodies on your screen?"

I have to inhale again at the words "dead bodies." I close my eyes for a moment, pressing my cold fingers to my temples to shoo away the nausea.

"Sure you want to know?"

"Well, I haven't eaten any of the sushi yet, so if I hurl, it'll at least be quick," I grumble. I fight the urge to cross my arms like a petulant teenager. I don't like being left out of the important stuff just because I have the weakest stomach in a twenty-mile radius.

Zoe smirks at me. "Good point. Plus, it'd be such a waste of good food. Give me just a sec. I have an idea."

I wait, back turned to the desk with Zoe just visible in my periphery. She's typing away, fingers flying across the keyboard and eyes scanning the screen faster than a normal human's should.

A few seconds pass and then she slides out of the chair and gestures for me to sit.

"I cut things a bit. Just pretend you're looking at cross-stitch or something."

There's a brief hesitation before I sputter, "What?"

"Just sit down, Kar."

I shake my head, doing as she says, and wincing as she turns the chair to face the screen.

It's not as bad as I thought it'd be. There are still two pictures up. Two disturbingly-close-to-skin-looking images, but they aren't the whole bodies. And if I concentrate, I can pretend I'm looking at stamps on a leather purse.

"What *is* that?" I lean in for a better look at the stamp-looking marks. There is one on each image, clearly a burn of some kind, but entirely unhealed.

It looks like an eye. Or part of an eye, at least. The somewhat almond shape and a partial circle within. The vertical line through it all could be an iris... if someone was drawing in a really weird style.

"Great question," Zoe murmurs. The sound of gears turning in her brain is almost audible.

I grab a notepad from the side of her desk and ask for a pencil. She pulls one from a neatly stacked set of plastic boxes each holding a different writing utensil. My fingers are quick, sketching the design before my stomach realizes what I'm really looking at.

Just like the way it works when I'm writing things down.

Despite the concern about up-chucking, curiosity gets the better of me as I draw.

"Who are they?" I ask in a low voice.

"The informant." Zoe mimics my quiet. "Stretch. And that butcher's kid. The one SAL talked to who used to be in their family."

"SAL?" I ask.

"Stares A Lot." She sounds more exasperated than she should, given that literally *no one* would be able to figure that out from the clues.

But Nick *does* stare at her a lot. "Right," I say, turning my attention back to my sketch. "So, the butcher's kid. He's the WITSEC guy."

"But not," Zoe corrects. "He claims the feds had nothing to do with it. He took off 'cause someone at the top of the family chain killed his kid."

I set down the pencil and turn from the screen. "Right. And judging by this," I gesture to the zoomed in bodies, "there's a good chance it was the same person who killed Stretch."

She nods. "Which means SAL is in just as much danger as we assumed."

I push back from the desk, earning an eyebrow raise as Zoe's chair snags on the carpet. "What could Stretch have known to get him killed, though? Surely his loyalty to the family would have kept him quiet."

Zoe shrugs, the movement morphing into a yawn as she eyes the sushi bag. "I don't think there's much counting on loyalty in *this* family. They put the patriarch behind bars. He's serving consecutive life sentences."

I heave a sigh and take her signal to head into the kitchen and pull down plates. She follows me, soft feet padding on the spotless linoleum.

Piles of sushi go on each of the simple white and gold designed plates (I took all the colorful ones when I moved in with Zack). Small sauce bowls are filled with an array of soy sauce, eel sauce, spicy mayo, and whatever it is they send with the gyoza that I cannot get enough of.

Because it's me, Zoe is fine with us eating in the kitchen. We lean against the counter, talking about the mundane things that get swept to the side when something like a murder investigation is underway.

There is something, though. Something about my best friend that is just a little off. I rinse my plate thoroughly before putting it in the dishwasher. The chopsticks and sauce bowls I clean by hand.

"You, uh," she says as I reach out for her plate. "You mentioned SAL was feeling irritable?"

I catch her gaze quicker than that one guy from Kung Fu is with the pebble. Her blue eyes meet mine for a brief second before she darts them away.

I inhale, easing my breath out slowly and aiming for nonchalant. "Yeah, he didn't like that I made the connection about his dad dying. I think it rattled him. And then there's the issue of him only having a few minutes to chat with Frank if he does end up calling the prison. He and Zack are putting together a game plan for if it comes to that."

She nods.

I clear my throat, scrubbing at a stuck piece of rice before it pops off the porcelain. "You guys had some time to talk yesterday, right? Before Zack and I got back. How'd that go?"

She squints at me.

"I'm just asking..." I close up the dishwasher and dry my hands on a clean towel hanging from the oven. "Because it seems like you have a lot in common."

Her scoff is overdone. A broadway actress trying to ensure the balcony seats understand the emotion.

I raise an eyebrow. "It's me, Zo. What's going on?"

She scowls. I cross my arms. We aren't going to get to the movie portion of the night until I get some answers out of her.

"I don't like him," she finally spits out.

I give her an incredulous look. She turns away from me, moving to the tiny pantry and yanking out an organic package of brownie mix.

"Get the butter, please," she growls.

I purse my lips.

Zoe ignores my lack of instruction-following. She zips around the kitchen, grabbing a glass bowl, an egg, butter, and her fancy glass-jar milk. Less than a minute later, the butter is melting in a shallow pan on the stove, the oven is preheating, and she's whisking like a mad-woman.

"Zoe."

She glances at me, something oddly close to fear in her gaze.

"You've gone on whole rants about strangers at coffee shops. Talk to me. What do you not like about our new mobster friend?"

Her lip curls. "TCT's friend. Not mine."

I shake my head lightly, stepping forward to click off the stove and pour the final ingredient into the brownie mix. "Try again," I say as I set the hot pan in the sink.

"It's like this feeling in my stomach." Zoe uses a claw-like hand to gesture toward her abdomen. The other hand still cradles the batter. "It's this clenching and wiggling, like snakes or something. It feels new and bad, and I hate it."

She slams the bowl onto the counter with more force than is necessary. With a furrowed glare aimed at the oven, she pours the mix into an 8x8 pan.

"Leave it to a guy to make me feel nauseated," she grumbles.

"Is it all bad?" I ask, taking the empty glass bowl and rinsing it out while she sprinkles chocolate chips into the batter. "The stomach feeling? Or is it some weird mix of bad and good?"

Her icy glare turns on me before she faces the counter again. In a quiet voice, she responds, "A mix, I guess. Good and bad, but still nauseating."

My eyes go wide for half a second before I smooth my features. As she waits for the oven, I pull a bottle of wine from the cabinet.

"Ahh." Aim for casual. I can't go head-on or she'll close up like a clam. "Is it just when you see him? When you're together? Or when you have to talk to him?"

I don't see her expression, but her response comes through gritted teeth. "All the time. Even when he's not there."

I stifle a chuckle at the frustration in her voice. "Yep," I mutter. "Sounds familiar." I reach for glasses next, pulling down her set of crystal with frosted geometric designs decorating the round parts.

"What?" The word lands hard and sharp, like she's already prepared to not like what I'm about to say.

I turn. "You're going to want some wine."

The oven beeps. She furrows her brow suspiciously. "What are you talking about?"

I set my glass down and step around her, gently easing the brownie mix onto the top rack while I steel myself to give my friend the hard truth.

The oven clicks closed, and I face her head-on. "You like him, Zoe. Like... *like like* him."

Zoe's eyes get bigger than I've ever seen. Alarm flashes across her face, and she clenches the stem of her wineglass with white knuckles. Her other hand reaches toward the counter, slender fingers closing around the handle of a knife in the butcher's block.

She's not holding it like she's about to cut into brownies, though. She's holding it like she just caught sight of a guy hitting his girlfriend.

"Woah!" I throw my hands up, quite concerned about the wild look on her usually calm face. "What are you gonna do? Kill him?"

She brandishes the blade; a lock of hair comes out of her ponytail. Her forehead beads with sweat. "Maybe!"

"Zoe." I approach her slowly.

She lowers the knife to her side, a startling amount of fear in her gaze.

I attempt a placating tone without sounding condescending. "This is *not* the appropriate response to a crush. Not everything is solved with murder."

She glares at me. "We literally have a list of things that have been solved with murder."

I roll my eyes. "You're having a full on Karrie style freak-out right now." I raise an eyebrow, struck with realization. "Is this what it looks like when I have a break-down?"

"No." Zoe scowls, setting the knife onto the counter and pressing her palm to her chest. "You don't hold a knife during a breakdown. You hold a toilet bowl."

"Wow." A humorless chuckle jumps from my lips. "Okay, that feels mean."

Thirty minutes later, we are curled up on the couch with second glasses of wine and hot brownies with vanilla ice cream in cute bowls on the coffee table. I have a grocery list made up for tomorrow. We are less than two days from New Years... which means I have champagne to buy—among other things—for the mini feast and party Zack and I are planning. Zoe reluctantly agreed to attend, with very strict rules about what I am and am not allowed to say with Nick in the room.

Psych plays idly in the background of our conversation, which has turned once again to the case.

"I still don't get why he went to see the Saint in the first place." Zoe shakes her head. "It was a stupid thing to do, and he's not stupid."

I grin, wiggling my eyebrows at her. She swats at me with the back of her hand.

"Seriously," she says. "The Sain betrayed him, right? Wasn't that the whole reason the man is in prison? Because he went against their one big rule?"

I sober, my mind dancing away to a few different conversations Zack and I have had about Zoe's understanding of family. Part of her not getting it comes from the way her mind works. And part of it comes from her having a whole, functioning family. As little as she sometimes cares about her parents, she *has* them. Always. In her corner, backing her up, loving her unconditionally.

I'm entirely positive that if she were someday caught, dragged into a courtroom, and put on trial, Mom and Dad would be right next to me, supporting her the whole way.

She doesn't have the perspective of someone like me or Zack or Nick. Someone whose parents preferred liquor or drugs or con-artistry over their kid. She knows I love her parents, but the depth of gratitude I feel for them, the depth of gratitude Nick feels for his uncle, is a little beyond her awareness.

"Nick's dad was kind of a shit-head," I say softly.

She hears the change in my tone and adjusts her focus. She gives a little nod.

I shrug. "From everything Zack and Nick have said, the man had big ambitions and zero follow-through. His failures in the family business led to drinking, drugs, prostitutes, you name it. There were more than a few times he left Nick alone in shady motel lobbies while he got his rocks off with someone or nearly OD'd by himself."

Zoe leans forward, setting her wine glass next to her bowl. "I didn't know about that."

I give half a shrug. "How could you? It's not like that's something a Google search would bring up. I only know so much because of Zack."

Not entirely true, but mostly.

"What does any of that have to do with Frank the Saint, though?" she asks.

I give her half a smile. "You remember all the shit my parents pulled, right?"

She nods.

"And how I had *you* waiting to take me in every time things got too bad?"

Anger clouds her expression for a second. She nods again.

"That was Frank for Nick. He was the oldest of the siblings, the patriarch of the family, watching his little brother be an absolute failure of a father. He took Nick in. Protected him, kept him warm and clothed and fed... he was like a dad to him."

Zoe hisses an exhale through her teeth. "So putting him away..."

"Was really fucking hard," I say with a nod. "And I'm betting the anniversary of Nick's *real* dad's death sparked a lot of repressed emotions. Whether Nick wants to admit that or not."

"Shit."

I nod. "Shit, indeed."

We lean in, Zoe patting my leg as I lay my head on her shoulder. A few minutes of shenanigans happen on the screen before I straighten and reach for my melty ice cream brownie bowl.

"I'm really glad I have you, Zo. For all the times you've saved me as an adult, but even more for what you gave me as a kid."

She flushes, grabbing her wine and dessert as well and retreating to her corner of the couch. "And what was that?"

I smile, returning my gaze to the TV to avoid embarrassing her further. "A family."

Chapter Twelve

KISS OR BARF

I've been in learning mode since my discussion with Karrie, soaking in tidbits I've paid little attention to over the years. But since this is the first real, healthy relationship Karrie's ever had where I've genuinely liked the man she's with, I'm studying the things they do with an academic lens.

Coming to terms with *liking* another human being in *that way* has been a process. I went through the five stages of grief in the last two days, camping out in the anger stage for longer than the others.

I spent my hours of rage chopping vegetables instead of the humans Karrie seems to think I enjoy killing.

She's reaping the fruits of my enraged labor as she and TCT get a stir-fry going for our New Year's Eve dinner. I watch them with calculated appraisal, noting the way her hands slide across his body when they maneuver around each other, or how he looks at her with affection in his gaze as he sings along to Ain't No Mountain High Enough that plays softly on the radio. Sometimes she'll grin at him and join in, her off-key alto pulling him flat as well.

SAL is watching them, too, but his eyes are on their hands as they handle the food. I swear he twitches when Karrie reaches out to touch the handle on the wok after she's just diced a piece of raw chicken. But I know Karrie, and I've trained her well. She stops herself and washes her hands thoroughly—twice—before she touches anything else.

It's odd. His hyper-vigilance about it irritates me, and I realize it's because I'm bothered he doesn't trust Karrie. So, apparently, even when I *like* someone, I'm going to put Karrie first.

I tip my head, considering that. I wonder how amenable he will be to being second-place in my life. Because there's no doubt in my mind that he's interested in me romantically. That body language thing. And, duh, I'm a catch. He's no slouch, for sure.

That weird fluttering discomfort goes through my stomach like it has whenever I think about him like that. I'm not sure that equates to much beyond companionship at the moment, and even that is a big maybe.

The idea of another human touching me, other than a hug from my most loved and trusted people (literally three humans), has been repulsive to me from my earliest memories. But when I think about the human doing the touching being Nick Farelli...

That certainly *doesn't* make me want to pull a Karrie-during-a-murder-investigation barfing session, which is proof enough of the insanity of the situation.

But what is it that draws me to him? He's good at cleaning and research? But TCT is clean and getting better at the routine every day, and though I'll never admit it to him directly, Tom is killer at research and piecing things together. And arguably, Tom is a good-looking guy. Physical attraction is a must for long-term companionship according to most academic journals.

Maybe it's the murder thing.

I tip my head again, listening to Karrie and Tom's off-key duet as they get louder and then start laughing when they mess up the same line of the song. I'm not looking at them anymore. I'm staring at SAL as he winds tighter. The two lovebirds clearly aren't paying as much attention to what they're doing as he thinks they should be, and his unease threatens to pull a smile out of me.

Definitely the murder thing. Has to be.

Uncharted fucking territory to find a man endearing. I can't help vacillating between hating what this does to me and being absolutely fascinated by the change since coming to the acceptance phase of my grief journey.

But because SAL has been wound up since arrival—according to Karrie, who got her intel from Tom—SAL has not been handling the news well that his aborted visit to his uncle in prison triggered the order for his execution.

I can see it, too. Not just in the hawk-like way he watches Tom and Karrie's dinner prep, but the fact that he's wiped down all the surfaces in the room multiple times. His germophobia stems from emotional anxiety, whereas mine comes from too much knowledge about the disgusting world around us.

I'd offer him a distraction, but what I have to discuss with him isn't going to make his concern any better about his status with his family. A theory has been blooming in my mind about what it is I've discovered, but the only person who can confirm my suspicion is the man whose legs are being assaulted by my attention-whore cat, to no avail.

Mac's affection for this man is the clincher I hadn't known it would be.

"Hey, S—uh, Nick."

He turns his gaze to me immediately, and I gesture for him to join me on the couch while I lug my laptop from the desk to my lap.

Without question, he scoops the cat up with an easy fluidity, like he's been doing it for years. Something squeezes in my chest when I see him cradle Mac like a little baby.

My heart. It's my heart that's squeezing. Or maybe it's growing—like the Grinch. Or maybe I'm having an aortic aneurysm.

What the hell is happening to me?

That's called falling in love, a voice that sounds suspiciously like Karrie says in my head, and I glance at her just to make sure she hasn't telepathically sent me the message. She's busy feeding a morsel of food to TCT as if she isn't still waiting for an answer to an incredibly important question.

But this is what it means to love someone. Right? My capacity to forgive or overlook is pretty deep when it comes to her. Would I be able to enjoy time with Nick in the same situation?

SAL settles next to me, scratching under Machete's chin.

"I have something interesting to show you," I say, noting the careful tone I can't help from using.

He hears it, too, because his body tightens in anticipation.

I lift a hand hesitantly and pat his thigh in reassurance. And then I pull the hand away, frowning as I look down at it. My palm tingles from that brief touch.

"Um, right," I say, shaking my head before turning to the laptop. I pull up the zoomed-in pictures I cropped while showing them to Karrie. "So, I did some digging about the Butcher's son's death while I was waiting on Stretch's autopsy."

"Digging," SAL repeats, raising one thick brow in skepticism.

"I'm a good... digger."

He gives me a sly smile, something small and subtle, but it's there, which means he isn't fooled. But if anyone is familiar with illegal "digging," it'd be a mafia guy.

"Anyway," I drawl. "Once Stretch's autopsy became available, I found something interesting."

I pull in a slow breath and hold it while I turn the laptop to SAL. His hand under Mac's chin stills as his dark eyes become slits. A hardness takes up residence in his expression, and I can tell he recognizes what we're looking at.

"You know what it is, don't you?"

He doesn't move, even as Mac shifts and moves in his arms, annoyed that his pets stopped. "It's Frank's calling card. Something only he did."

"Both of these were done in the last five years. As in, while Frank the Saint's been locked up." I watch his face for a reaction, but there's not much that gets past his mask of calm.

Except his eyes. I can see his wheels turning behind the dark brown sharpness as he's processing. "He couldn't have done it."

It's what I'd suspected, and the eagerness to get to the bottom of this part of the mystery has electricity building inside of me. "So who did? Who else knows about this, Nick?"

He finally looks at me, and my stomach does that gross and exhilarating flipping thing, and I can't decide if I want to kiss him or throw up on him.

"Only three people knew it was Frank's," he says. "Everyone else just knew it was bad news because that mark meant someone was out to get them. That's why the butcher took off with the rest of his family."

Even though I have my suspicions about what three people knew, I'm frustrated that he won't come out and say it. Is it some sort of mafia training not to list names in case someone's listening?

"What three people?"

"Carlotta, Georgie, and me."

There's a ripple of hurt in those simple words, and I find myself mulling that over more than the possible suspects he's just listed. I sift through Karrie's explanation when I told her I couldn't fathom why he'd go see the Saint in prison after his betrayal of the family.

"What if it wasn't the Saint who did it?" I speak quietly, knowing that this is likely another item on a list of family disappointments.

Nick shakes his head. "No one else would know how to do it."

I scoff, luring his gaze to my face again. "It couldn't be that hard to figure out."

His expression darkens to a scowl, and I realize I've offended him. "I know it looks simple, but there are some unique things about it that are hard to emulate. And only someone taught directly by him would know."

His eyes flicker away at that. There's pain in the languid brown, and it makes me consider the other possibilities.

"Could there be a copycat?"

He turns to study the images again, and he's quiet for a long time as he mulls it over. "Possibly. It's fucking ballsy to copy it in the first place."

"Have you ever tried?"

He jerks his head to look at me like he's startled I'm there. "Never. It was a respect thing. I was…" He swallows. I would've missed the reaction if I didn't catch the way his throat bobs. "I was waiting for him to teach me."

I grow very still, sensing the agony in his words, though they're spoken so evenly, anyone listening wouldn't pick up on it. I want to catch each of his words and hold them in my hands, put them under a microscope to compare them to the tiny movements of his face. I want to dissect everything he says and understand them.

And then I jolt at that realization.

How bizarre to want to understand someone like this.

"Frank's betrayal hurt you deeply," I say, watching what that verbal acknowledgement does to his expression.

He glances toward the kitchen where Tom and Karrie are still cooking and flirting shamelessly. "He always treated me like I was the son he never had. So when he said no kids, no trafficking, I was proud to adhere to that code. It's honorable. Right." He pauses. "He deserved to go down for going back on the code."

Anger now, a cold, brittle sound that glints in his tone. His eyes darken, brows creeping low. I don't think I will ever grasp how much that must grieve him, but something stirs in my chest. A need to protect and make someone pay for this pain.

"You believe strongly in that code," I say.

"Kids are off-limits. I don't care who you are, I don't hurt your kid." He shakes his head. "My dad was as shitty as they come. Didn't care what happened to me as long as he got his next score. He would've sold me for a hit of crack if given the chance. That's why Frank took me away from him."

I look over at Karrie, remembering the times she'd come to my house when we were kids because her mom never came home and there'd been no food in their house. Middle school was when she'd basically moved in with us because my parents refused to let her go home, even when Hilary came around looking for her.

"He OD'ed."

His dad, I realize.

"Anyway, finding out the man I trusted and followed blindly could be such a hypocrite..." SAL shakes his head.

I take a slow breath, knowing this has led him to dark thoughts. But my next question will add to the bleeding wound, and I regret my need for the answer. "Is it possible he taught someone else the mark?"

SAL's mouth turns down, little lines forming to cradle the corners of his lips.

I'm momentarily distracted by his lips and how they look somewhat pillowy for a man's. Would that make them soft?

"It's possible. I thought it would be me, but..." He shrugs.

"Prima Donna?" I suggest, shaking myself from my bizarre thought process.

"Carlotta would be most likely since she's his actual daughter. But Farellis don't do kids. She's spoken out against it more times than I can count, especially since Frank went to prison for it."

I don't point out how words don't always mean truth. He probably can't take another round of betrayal from someone so close to him. But that makes me wonder about Prima Donna ordering a hit on him, if she's indeed the one who did. "Do you think she believes you went to the Saint because you're thinking of going against the code, too?"

His brows rise, and I can tell he thinks it's a very possible scenario. "Trust has been shaky between us all since he went down."

I suck a breath through my teeth. "Shaky enough to order a hit on you even at the slight possibility?"

He tips his head. "The family has killed for less."

I turn his words over in my head, analyzing the tone. "So now we need to find out who ordered it."

He glances at me, his eyes tightening like he's measuring me. "Maybe I should go straight to Frank. Talk to him for real."

My brows dance upward. "You sure?"

He lifts a shoulder. "He either knows something or he's got something to do with this. Maybe he taught someone how to do his carving."

Karrie makes a gagging sound, alerting me that she and Tom have joined us in the living room.

My head snaps in her direction. "Don't barf on my carpet, Kar. I love you, but I just had it steam cleaned."

She shoots me a glare.

"Did you say you're going to go visit Frank?" TCT asks, his brows steepling in concern. "Is that really a good idea?"

"I need some answers," SAL says very softly. It seems almost too calm, and I wonder just how much of his emotions are roiling just below the surface.

"Wasn't your last visit the reason you're here?" Karrie asks between her deep breathing.

SAL doesn't reply.

"Frank the Saint can't kill him inside a prison," I point out. "And he's the one who taught our murderer his mark, so that's a guaranteed answer."

"But he might be the one who wants Nick dead!" Karrie leans forward, her face flushing with the color she'd lost a moment before. "And who's to say someone won't be waiting to take him out as soon as he walks out the door?"

"That's why he's not going alone." I say, pulling three sets of eyes in my direction.

Karrie's narrow on my face. "You are *not* going into a mafia den with McMurder Pants."

"McMurder Pants?" SAL murmurs to himself.

I open my mouth to argue, but Tom's hands shoot up. "I'll go with him."

Karrie whirls on him. "You will *not*."

Tom looks like a chagrined little kid, and I'm grinning, enjoying Bossy Karrie. And then my smile drops off because she's told me about how much Tom likes Bossy Karrie and exactly when she pulls that out.

Now *I* might actually barf.

"I have a contact in the FBI," Tom continues, making his case. "If I go, I can see what he knows about these new developments in the family. They've always got eyes on the crime syndicates."

Karrie is already shaking her head, though Nick is looking speculative.

"How about we all go?" I suggest, still swallowing down the bile that threatened. "Strength in numbers."

Karrie turns to me with a growing smile, and it's like a light has gone on in her eyes as her face transforms. "Ooooh, a trip?" She brings her hands together. "I'm planning all the activities!"

"It's not a vacation, Kar," I remind her.

She shuts her eyes, freezing her brittle smile in place. "Don't take away my fun or the distraction it is to plan a spa day instead of thinking about someone carving into—*hrmph*—dead bodies." She presses a fist to her mouth for a moment. "Spa day," she repeats like a mantra.

I look at SAL to gauge his thoughts on the situation because I'm not sure a few hours at the spa is his jam. I would guess, though, that he's rolling through the possibility of getting face-to-face with Frank again, not the idea of a stranger touching him. I shudder at the thought, myself. Might have to pass on the spa day.

I try to imagine what it might mean for him to talk with the surrogate father who betrayed the family. Walking through the memories of Karrie's struggle to release her grief over her shitty parents, I have some sense of what it means to have someone step in, only to have them betray you.

Griller basically became that for Karrie, and I can't even picture him doing anything to hurt her. But the thought of him betraying her makes my skin heat with anger already.

Karrie and TCT have moved across the room, and she's taken my laptop to start looking at flights and hotels.

But as I sit next to SAL, who's so still I'd think he's stopped breathing, I put my hand in his. It's as much to comfort him as an experiment on touching another human who's not my sister in all but blood. He squeezes my hand but doesn't react in any other way. The contact *doesn't* make my skin crawl, though that might be because I know how often this man washes his hands.

I bet he never leaves a shred of evidence behind when he eliminates people.

Another little flip happens in my stomach like it's trying out for the Olympic gymnastics team, and I press my lips together.

I make a note to ask Karrie if that means I'm going to throw up or kiss a man.

CHAPTER THIRTEEN

MISSION IMPOSSIBLE

My fingers fly across the keyboard. Zoe can kill people without leaving a trace. Zack's true crime podcast is sensitive to families and enticing to listeners. Nick... I don't know... is probably great at polishing windows or something... and definitely glaring.

But me? I'm absolutely fantastic at planning trips.

A lot of other things, too, but right now, with Nick and Zoe sitting close and discussing his family issues (we finally met someone who had a more messed up upbringing than me), and Zack over my shoulder, one hand resting comfortably on my arm, I feel the desire to show off my skills.

It's New Year's Eve and, though Zoe lightly protested, I managed to decorate her apartment appropriately to launch us into a new year. Gold streamers hang from the windows. I brought pull crackers full of cat toys, a bottle of champagne, a very expensive box of hand crafted chocolates, and four of Zoe's favorite yearly pocket planners—one for each of us.

I'm tempted to pull mine out now, to begin jotting down the list of ideas I have for our *Epic Mob/Spa Seattle Adventure* or EMSSA as I've affectionately named the trip.

Because it's New Year's Eve, there is no logic behind jetting off to uncover Nick's awful family secrets immediately. We will have to wait a couple of days for flights to cool down—for both price and capacity.

I click the final button to purchase four tickets. Direct flight, not too early in the morning, for the 3rd of January. Hotels are next, and I cast an evil grin toward the couple on the couch before I get two adjoining rooms. One with a King-sized bed. One with two Queens.

Oh no, I'll say when we check in, *they must have run out of double queen rooms... I suppose Zack and I should share the big bed. And you two can...*

My chuckle is audible. I stifle it. The thought of Zoe and Nick sharing a hotel room—if not a bed—sends a giddy buzz through my bloodstream.

My best friend, my sister, is having *feelings* for someone. For the first time in her life. She was there for me through every crush, every craving, every emotional onslaught brought about by relationships. I never thought I'd get to be there for her in this way.

I glance back at the killers on the couch. Zoe is half-bent, her expression serious and oddly compassionate as she speaks to Nick in a low voice. The mafia man is cradling

Mac like a baby, absently giving scritches under the kitty's chin as he responds in an equally quiet murmur.

"I'm glad they're getting along," Zack whispers in my ear.

The warm feel of his breath on my skin distracts me for a moment. We've shared a lot of kisses since basically making up after he went to rescue Nick. That's about all we've shared in the physical touch department, though.

A multitude of things are in our way. The first, Nick staying at our apartment. The man is so constantly on alert. And, while I have plenty of kinks, voyeurism isn't one of them.

Beyond company, the unsettled question of engagement lingers like a cold shower between us. Singing and dancing in the kitchen, sharing tender hugs and kisses, and giggling together as we watch Nick and Zoe fight falling for each other, is the extent of our passions at the moment.

I reach up, cupping his cheek with a hand before gesturing to Zoe's laptop screen. "This look like a good one?"

He leans in and scrolls through a few pictures. He blanches. "How much is this?"

I grin. "Not as much as you'd think. Ya girl knows how to find the best deals."

"I should have figured that. Yeah, it looks great." Zack's lips land on my forehead, soft and warm and comforting.

I click another button, my credit card collecting points as I plan on us being in Seattle for four nights. Then I shift in the chair, tilting my head to meet Zack's gaze.

"After this," I point to the screen, "when Nick is safe and we know who has been killing people and we're back home... we need to talk about my question."

His throat bobs as he swallows. I don't want him to move away, but he does. A half-step back, probably so I don't have to tilt my head as much, but my heart aches at the space he's putting between us.

"Yeah," he murmurs. "Yeah, we will."

A few seconds pass, our eyes locked as I try to fathom—yet again—what could possibly be holding him back.

There is something like guilt hiding in the furrow of his brow, but is it because he hasn't answered yet, or because he knows his answer will destroy me?

I turn away, back to the laptop, to continue planning. Another moment later and Zack walks away, retreating to the kitchen.

"... and that's it!" I clap my hands in excitement, finishing off my summary of our travel plans.

Despite any level of frustration in the back of my mind, I can't deny that this trip will be an adventure.

"EMSSA?" Nick's slightly dumbfounded voice does nothing to lessen my enthusiasm.

"EMSSA," I say with a nod.

Zoe laughs.

Zack laughs.

Nick looks pained.

"Now," I wave a hand dramatically at the laptop now positioned on the coffee table. "It's a minute until midnight. The New Year is almost upon us. Zoe?"

I turn to my friend, who shakes her head with a smile and pops the cork on the champagne (a job only she is allowed to do because of the threat of spillage). We pass glasses around and, as the clock ticks nearer to midnight, even Nick joins in the fun.

Music blares out of the speakers. Mac prances in delight, scooting his new toys away from the areas of foot traffic.

Zack comes up to me, champagne glass in one hand, the other looping around my waist as he pulls me to him. I grin, the flutter in my chest and his strong arm holding me close reminders of the reasons I love him.

"Ten seconds," he murmurs playfully.

"Nine." I lick my lips.

"Eight."

"Gross," Zoe calls from across the room.

I giggle, pressing closer to Zack.

"Three," he whispers, breath tickling my nose.

"Two."

On one, we lock lips. He leans me back, the one arm all he needs to keep me sturdy in the passionate kiss.

"Bleh," Zoe's voice is nearer this time, her distaste colored with humor.

I reach blindly, setting my glass on the counter behind me, and wrapping my hands around his face to pull him even deeper into the kiss.

I feel his grin against my lips. He knows I'm going harder to mess with Zoe.

"Hey, remember that time you sliced a guy open with a steak knife? Blood all over the place?"

I lurch away from Zack as my stomach flips in a very pukey way.

"Don't *do* that!" I snap. I make a "hrmph" sound as I hold in my dinner, pressing my fist to my mouth as everyone laughs. There is no irritation, though. Only love and continuing attempts to avoid hurling all over Zoe's carpet.

"Proudest moment of my life." Zoe sighs happily, a dreamy look coming over her face.

From the corner of my eye, I catch Nick's focused gaze soaking in every ounce of her smile.

That alone is enough to steady my stomach.

There have been plenty of men interested in Zoe over the years. Dozens, probably hundreds, but in my *life* I've never imagined she'd experience something even close to desire for another human being. We've kinda thought she was probably asexual since high school. Which did nothing to stop my teasing and light poking to get her to try out a relationship, but always with an undercurrent of understanding that it wasn't going to happen.

This, though...

Zoe's eyeline drifts, catching Nick's stare. The two of them make eye contact for a split second before each turns away. Zoe's cheeks take on a hue very similar to her lucky sweater. Nick's jaw clenches, his expression flustered before he catches me watching him.

I grin.

He turns away, lifting champagne to his lips.

My grin deepens. This trip is going to be strenuous. A talk with an imprisoned father figure, the possibility of a brief chat with the local FBI branch, and the looming threat of a mobster who wants to kill Nick over information he doesn't actually know...

But all of that pales in comparison to my actual task in Seattle. Getting Zoe and Nick to admit feelings.

I square my shoulders as Zack steps away to grab us some chocolates from the kitchen counter.

Mission accepted.

"EMSSA begins!" I twirl, my black skirt flaring out and my shoulder bag threatening to slam into Zack.

He takes a practiced step back with a laugh.

"Small airports are the best," he says with a look at Nick.

The grungy mafia man has done a complete flip. Something about going home, going to see Frank tomorrow, and possibly discovering the truth about who killed Stretch, triggered a serious revitalization in the man.

And damn, does he clean up nice.

Zoe hasn't been able to keep her eyes from drifting to him every few minutes, each time accompanied by her clenching her teeth and furiously looking elsewhere.

Nick's hair is trimmed, the shaggy look still present, but now more purposeful. His beard and mustache are short and neat. Fingernails filed. Suit shirt currently wrinkle-free, though I'm sure that will change after the plane-ride.

The four of us have just gotten through security. I got an extra pat-down, as usual. Zoe and the guys waited for me, and now we're all set to head to Seattle.

Nick's fake ID gave us no trouble getting through check-in. Zack's small airport comment has me briefly concerned about the return trip before I remember that Nick might not even be with us when we head back to Spokane in a few days.

The mundane conversation I usually love—people watching, weather, traffic, and the best method of sharpening blades—fades into the background as I contemplate Nick staying in Seattle. Re-upping his mafia life-style once his family gets sorted out.

Flying back to Spokane with Zoe beside me. Alone.

"Hey." Zack puts a hand on my shoulder. "You okay?"

I blink, turning to him with my brow furrowed and my eyes wide to keep tears from welling. "Is Nick coming back with us?"

He looks startled. A quick glance at our two friends across the way shows them in deep conversation. Nick mimes holding something, thrusting it forward. Zoe gives a nod of approval and speaks with more animation than she's ever used with anyone besides me.

"I don't know," he murmurs. Sadness licks at his tone. "I hadn't actually thought about it."

"The mystery has you distracted."

He nods with a grin.

"Distracted from a lot of things," I say, unable to keep the melancholy from my voice.

His face falls. "Kar..."

"Yeah." I lick my lips, rubbing my hands together before pulling my journal out of my bag. "I know. We'll talk when everything is sorted."

CHAPTER FOURTEEN

HOTEL NOT-PANICKING

I f I were the panicking type, I'm sure this constricting feeling in my chest, the irregular heart rate, and dry mouth might make me believe I am, indeed, panicking.

But I'm totally not.

Because *he's* not.

SAL—the Cannoli—Nick—is looking so calm it's asinine as we ride the elevator up to the fourth floor where our rooms are. And Karrie looks downright giddy.

Of course she does. She gets to snuggle right up to Tom and probably do whatever he's clearly thinking about doing because he's got the most devilish smile on his face.

So unprofessional. We're here for a case. Which is exactly why I'm *not* panicking.

Except I'm going to be sharing a room with Nick, who still stares a lot, but I can't bring myself to think of him this way anymore because now so do I. Uncontrollably. I am officially a Stares A Lot, too.

I could literally share a room with any other man and have zero feelings about the fact, aside from disgust. I'd carry on as if he didn't exist. But this is *Nick*, the cannoli *with* substance that I might actually want to eat. I can't stop wondering what it would be like to kiss him. What if I accidentally do it? I'm a scientist. The compulsion to test out hypotheses is wired into my DNA.

I've watched Karrie kiss plenty of guys, and aside from it being one of the most repulsive things to witness, my mechanical knowledge of the process is burned into my brain from my thorough analysis.

Yes, at one point, she had me observe her adventures so I could break down her technique, and she could improve upon it. There's a reason these guys always come back for more.

I know exactly *how* to do it.

I've just never wanted to.

But now I'm getting curious. The beginning of an experiment always stems from curiosity, from wondering what might happen if...

And the wondering starts with his lips. They look so soft, and theories about how they'd feel start swirling in my mind, especially since he's trimmed his beard and hair. And there's something about what he's wearing. It's done something to me, and I look at him without my permission no less than eight million times in the two minutes it takes to arrive at our floor.

I want to go back to the airplane, where we'd easily fallen into a continued discussion of knives—the ideal shape and size for concealment, how to maintain the appropriate sharpness. He introduced me to the brand he prefers because it's untraceable. Something produced for someone in his line of work. Not that I ever expected the mafia to be quite so careful about that sort of thing. I'd always thought they were pretty sloppy.

But Nick is anything but sloppy.

Dear God, what that thought does to me. He's the least sloppy person on the planet with his crisp clothes, his adherence to strict hygiene protocols, and the casual way he talks to me, like we've been doing this for years. Something stirs in my stomach, something warm and languid and unsettling as hell.

The elevator doors spring open, and I almost sprint out before I catch myself and simply step out to wait for the rest of them to disembark. My brain has started shorting out because of the proximity of Nick's body to mine.

And now I'm thinking about his body. *Motherfucker*.

I swallow at the possibility of accidentally getting a glimpse. I wait for my stomach to revolt against the idea, for my mind to recoil, for the revulsion to quell the panic that I'm pretending not to feel.

It doesn't happen.

The theories start swirling again. The hypothesis is that a man as fastidious as Nick would likely have a very meticulously curated physique. Knowing how long and lean he looks in that fitted button down and vest, I know there's probably no spare ounces of fat on him.

I spin on my heel as soon as everyone's out into the hall, and I lead the way to our rooms, one with a king-sized bed and one with two queens, a lockable door joining the rooms. Thank God Karrie volunteered to take the king bed. Not that she wouldn't. It made the most sense to give us the two queens and have the couple that lives together take the one bed.

We get to our respective doors, and while Nick holds the keycard to the lock on ours, panic sails up my throat like bile, and I jerk toward Karrie.

She notes my movement and turns, picking up on my terror immediately. Her mouth pops open. "Since we need to coordinate a few things, let's open the inner door to discuss what needs to happen while we get settled."

Tom's brows lower over his eyes as he looks at her, pushing their door open. But he shrugs. "Makes sense. I have to call my FBI contact first, but we can make a game plan once that's done."

Nick says nothing as he holds the door open for me to go first, and I scoot past him, studiously keeping my eyes forward.

I sweep the room and wonder if Nick has one of those black lights to check the cleanliness. This is one of those scenarios where I don't think I want to know. I want to pretend this is hospital sterile, and everything in this room is brand new.

Since it's not, though, I did cover some of my bases by bringing my own sheets.

Nick freezes in the act of wiping down the desk to watch as I start stripping the bed I've decided on for myself—the one closest to the exit.

He doesn't ask as I lug the pile of sheets to the small closet in the corner of the room and dump them inside. But he tips his head as I start yanking the sheets from my bag—the extra one I almost had to check because the flight had been more full than anticipated.

Understanding glimmers in his dark eyes, and something like admiration fills them. "I wish I'd thought of that."

"We could buy a new set for you while we're here," I suggest.

He considers but a knock on the connecting door keeps him from answering. I cross the room and flip the lock.

Karrie's smile is way too bright when it swings open. I'm not sure what she was expecting, but it's not this, apparently. Maybe she thought she'd find me curled into a ball in the corner. Or she hoped to catch us in the act of making out.

Blech.

I narrow my eyes. Too far, I think. For the moment, anyway. Gotta test the lips theory first. Perhaps I'll find them too squishy and unappealing.

Karrie's expression pinches when she realizes what she's interrupted. "Zoe, did you bring your own sheets?" She sounds offended. "I specifically picked this hotel because of its strict cleaning guidelines."

"You can never be too sure." I toss a casual hand in the direction of the half-made bed. "They're my least favorite set, so I can throw them out when we leave, and I can sleep better knowing I'm the only one who's ever slept on them."

"Genius," Nick murmurs from across the room.

Karrie shakes her head like I'm a mildly exasperating child. "How's it going in here otherwise?" She shoots her eyes to Nick and back to me, even though I am clearly feeling more in control now.

Because this is an experiment. Just a testing of theories.

"Fine. Might need to run out and get a new set of sheets for Nick," I reply.

I see him nod thoughtfully in my periphery.

"So, it's Nick, now, is it?" Karrie mutters to me.

I shoot her a look.

She sighs. "We can do that when we go grab dinner. Zack is on his call to the FBI guy. We'll do food and figure out the plan when he's done."

I move back to my bed to finish getting my sheets in place. "Sounds good."

Karrie moves with me, her eyes on Nick as he starts wiping down every door handle and knob and touchable surface. "We can leave that door open all night if you want," she whispers to me, tucking one corner of the fitted sheet under the mattress while I do the other.

I glance up. "I'll be fine. I can take him if he tries anything."

Karrie gives me a sly grin. "I don't think him trying anything is what had that panicked look in your eyes, Zo."

I glare at her but don't respond when Nick walks back from the bathroom, where he presumably sanitized every surface. I could get used to this kind of team work.

"Hey, Kar?" Tom sticks his head into the room, his phone tucked against his ear.

She heads back into their room to confer with him, and I finish tucking my sheets.

Nick pulls a pack of those little booties realtors have for house showings from his bag and tosses them on his bed.

"What are those for?" I ask.

He glances at the booties then shrugs. "I never walk into unknown situations without them. You never know when you need to cover your tracks. Or protect your shoes."

I've always been pretty thorough with my kills, but they almost always take place outside where trace evidence is harder to separate out with so much foot traffic. But it's...

"Smart."

He smirks, pulling out his box of nitrile gloves and another package of wipes that hasn't been opened yet. I'm just waiting for the hand sanitizer to—and there it is.

I grin and turn away, but I know Nick's eyes are on me. I can feel the speculation as it traces over my skin.

"You don't use booties," he says. It's not a question. "But you've never been caught."

I turn and place a hand on my hip. My cropped, baby pink sweater brushes the edge of my thumb. "Your little booties aren't the only thing keeping you from getting caught."

He rolls his eyes. "I know. I just mean, for someone as calculated as you are, I'm surprised you don't use them." He taps the box with a smidge of affection.

I laugh. "Well, murder isn't my *job* like it is yours. It's more of a...side gig." I wave my hand. "And I'm retired, anyway." I tip my chin toward Karrie and Tom in the other room.

"Zack's passed muster, then." He narrows his eyes, but he's doing that smirk thing—the one I like against my will. "You only do men, then?"

I snort. "Obviously. Why would I ever need to kill a woman? They don't tend to do the kind of shit men do."

He lifts a shoulder. "I've done plenty of women."

"Me too!" Karrie says brightly, clearly not aware of the topic of conversation as she comes back into the room.

Nick and I stare at each other as Karrie hops onto my bed like it's some sort of slumber party.

"What's your body count?" I ask, ignoring the way she grins and looks between us.

"Just women?" he asks, his knuckles brushing the surface of the desk in front of him.

I level him with a hard look. "Total."

He hesitates like he's worried I won't like his answer. "Several dozen, probably," he hedges. "I don't keep a tally."

Bullshit, I want to say, but I don't. There's no way a guy like him doesn't keep track. Not that it matters that much what the number is.

"I've lost count, too," Karrie muses, head bobbing.

I don't want to burst her bubble and clarify what the conversation is really about. She's probably still stuck on the fact that I *like* him to realize we're talking homicide instead of sexual conquests.

"What's yours?" Nick asks as the silence stretches, his lids going half-mast.

Karrie goes still, realization probably dawning.

"Much lower than yours," I shoot him a coy smile but check Karrie's progress through understanding.

She takes a breath, face twisting. "We're—*hrmph*—not talking about the same thing."

I pat her back. "No, we're not. But I am curious if he's done as many women as you have."

Tom's head pops around the edge of the door, his brows nearly touching his hairline. "Say, what, now?" Way too interested, though, hopefully he makes the same mistake Karrie did initially about what the actual topic is.

Karrie shuts her eyes and shakes her head, and I laugh to break some of the tension.

"Meeting set?" Nick asks, stuffing his hands into his pockets.

Tom's eyes drag from Karrie's pale face to Nick. "Uh, yeah. Unfortunately, the only time he had available is during visiting hours at the prison."

Nick's mouth twists, gaze going to the floor. He waves a dismissive hand. "That's alright. I can go alone."

There's a pinch in my chest, and tingles shoot into my fingertips. Some invisible force almost makes me step forward. Instead, words fall out of my mouth. "You can, but you won't."

Nick's eyes flash to my face, brows quirking in question.

"I'll go with you." I shrug, trying to pass it off as the most casual thing. But more nerves are firing inside of me at going somewhere with Nick than that first time I took a person's life. Like, I could literally describe my first murder in disturbing detail without batting an eye. Thinking about being alone-alone with Nick makes me bat a fucking eye, though. I can feel my left lid threatening to twitch.

"Karrie can go with Tom," I add, realizing it's been really quiet. "Buddy system."

I can practically hear Karrie squealing inside her own head. I don't have to look at her to know her naturally big eyes go as round as beach balls, and she's probably biting her lips together to keep from saying a thing, or she's grinning like an idiot. It's the look she always gets when we watch a new rom-com, and the couple hits that change in the relationship before the first kiss.

Instead of giving her a warning look, I just ignore her completely.

"Sounds like that works out, then." Tom claps his hands together then looks at Nick. "You'll be okay, man?"

Nick doesn't take his eyes from my face. "Yep. That works great."

CHAPTER FIFTEEN

C**OO**L

*C**ool, calm, collected.* Another chanted mantra in my head as Zack and I approach one of Seattle's FBI offices. Apparently this city is big enough for more than one. Though, as we get closer I realize this is maybe more of an under-the-radar office. There are no signs, no big windows into a fancy lobby, and no overly starched suits walking around.

I school my features, aiming for the *cool, calm, collected* mask I see on Zoe all the time. Except, of course, when she's within striking distance of Nick. Because it's looking more and more like kissing distance the longer they spend time together.

Thinking about the two unabashed murderers in my life has me losing track of my mantra. We are about to walk into a building full of people who'd love to get their hands on a serial killer and a mob enforcer. I need to be *sharp*.

"Relax, Karrie," Zack murmurs. His hand tightens around mine. My palms are sweaty, making our interlaced fingers slippery. "This is a quick check in. I'm going to give some info to my guy and hopefully we can get something in return."

I nod. "I don't like the idea of telling them anything about our friends."

He frowns at me, that glint in his eye stirring both lust and concern in my gut. "What are we telling them about Zoe?"

"Nothing, but she's with Nick." I raise an eyebrow, attempting to maintain steady breathing despite both my nerves and the speed of our pace.

"Right."

He leaves it there, but, as usual these days, unspoken words hang in the air between us.

Zack pushes the door open, and we step into the weird 70s wood-style lobby of what appears to be a dingy office building. Not exactly what I'd expect to see from my tax-payer dollars at work.

"Can I help you?" A brusque-looking woman with frizzy brown hair and a tan suit stares at us from behind a crescent-shaped desk. Behind her, protected by the pen in her hand and the numerous figurines just visible on the other side of her computer, is a set of doors that must lead to a hall of elevators.

I step forward with a smile, ready to pull out my extrovert charm, but Zack is a step ahead.

"We have an appointment," he says, tugging the flap on his bag and pulling out his wallet. He hands over an ID.

I do the same. The woman eyes them both with a suspicious air, then returns them and picks up the old phone on her desk.

"Richards," she snaps into the speaker. "You have an appointment. Come collect them." She hangs up and gives us another glare. "He'll be out in a moment. Have a seat."

As expected. I can't imagine they let anyone wander around here. Zack and I head over to the beige pleather couch and settle in to wait.

"Think they're doing okay?" I twist the butterfly ring on my thumb. It was an anniversary present from Zack. Dark wings drape across my knuckle.

Zack watches my movements, his gaze glued to the way the ring turns. "Yeah." His voice is distant. "I know Zoe has close to zero empathy, but I'm glad she's going with him. Nick has a tough exterior, but everything with Frank is really messing with his head."

I nod. "I can't imagine how it would feel if Zoe's mom or dad betrayed everything they taught me growing up."

He reaches over, hand closing around mine to ease the anxious fidgeting. I've made a red mark on my thumb from all the twisting.

"I'm really glad you introduced me to them," he murmurs. "I'm sorry the visit got cut short. It was nice to get a glimpse at your childhood."

I scoff and bump my shoulder into him.

"I mean it," he says with amused earnest. "You're a conundrum, Karrie Dunshire. It's nice to get to peel back the layers and see what makes you you."

A flutter in my chest somehow does the opposite of what I expect and, instead of feeling loved and cared for, I feel sadder than I was before.

"I still don't get Zoe, though." He shakes his head, unaware of my aching heart. "Does it seem like she and Nick have been getting along a little too well?"

I raise an eyebrow.

Zack scoots forward on the couch, a conspiratorial glint in his eye. "They spent the whole plane ride talking about knives. I know Zoe likes cooking, but that's a bit much, right?"

"Zack Lim. How the hell are ya?"

I exhale my nerves as a middle-aged balding man pushes through the doors to the back offices and greets Zack.

We stand. Zack shakes the man's hand and introduces me to Agent Richards. I flash a smile and shake his hand as well. I recognize his voice. Richards is a repeat interviewee on Armchair Detective. He likes to give his take on suspect interviews and police procedure. He often points out things people do wrong.

Richards leads us back, through the double doors, and down a stark hallway. His office door has a little plaque with his name on it. He gestures us inside and shuts the door.

His desk is metal, an old thing with an old phone, old computer, and enough dents to suggest Richards has slammed stuff into it a few times. The black swivel chair behind it is fraying. One of the seats in front of the desk is overstuffed and lumpy. The other is so threadbare I can almost see the springs.

I guess the 70s appearance of the lobby isn't just a cover.

Zack, always the gentleman, motions for me to take the lumpy chair. I opt for the other since I'll be perched on the edge anyway.

He gives me a grin as we settle in. Richards swings around his desk, cracks the blinds behind it to let in a little natural light, and plops into his chair.

"Back in Seattle, eh?" He gives Zack another wide grin. "What's dragged you back to the big city?"

Zack shifts his bag, pulling out his palm-sized investigator's notebook. "You heard about Stretch, right?"

Richards nods, his grin fading. "Yeah. Lotta shit going down with that family these days. Is that why you're back in town?"

I cast a glance at Zack. He looks at ease, not the bundle of nerves I am.

"Yep." Zack flips open the notebook. "I have some concerns about the old case. We've dug up a bit more info, and I'm worried we might not have put all the pieces together before Frank got put away."

Richards frowns. "Think so? We had more than enough evidence to bag him, Zack. Not to mention how quick the trial was. The prosecution, judge, and jury all knew what kind of scum he was in the first five minutes."

I shift, biting the inside of my cheek to keep my mouth shut. What he describes sounds like the opposite of a fair trial. And, mob boss or not, there are *some* things that should run the way they're supposed to.

Zack gives a muted sound of agreement, but his expression doesn't change. "My informant reached out after Stretch. They aren't entirely sure Frank was the one trafficking."

"He was found on the dock with a container of kids coming in from who-the-hell-knows-where," Richards snaps.

My eyes widen, throat catching as the details of Frank's arrest are finally thrown into the open.

"A..." My quiet voice is loud in the silence following Richards' outburst. "A 'container full of kids?'"

Zack gives the smallest nod of confirmation when I turn to look at him.

Richards scowls. "Our agency had been at odds with the Farelli family for years, but they became our top priority when we got the rundown on what Frank was up to. We organized a sting and caught the bastard red-handed."

I swallow. Zack shifts in his seat.

"I know, Richards, and I know what the evidence looked like. But Stretch was barely in the life. A two-bit thief who could never get a foot in the door with anything more serious. Why would someone go after him?"

He scoffs. "Simple. Someone is trying to take the big dog's spot. Trying to be like Frank and tie up loose ends."

"Who, though?" I ask, my voice soft. "And why go after Stretch unless he knew something? Maybe something that could exonerate Frank?"

"The whole family is fucked," Richards says. He leans back in his chair and folds his hands across his belly.

Zack raises an eyebrow. He puts his pen closer to the paper. "You're awfully calm for someone with a dead body in the morgue." He frowns. "You have a suspect."

I glance from the fed to my boyfriend. The whole point of this meeting is to get any intel Richards can provide. So far, that's not been much. But a fresh suspect could turn the whole case on its head.

Richards grins. "I do. Someone who was close enough to the man to want to try and fill his shoes. I know you had Stretch in your ear." He nods at Zack. "But we've got our own whispers from the inside."

My pulse races. "You have an informant in the family?"

He puffs up a bit. "Yeah, the same person who gave us the goods on Frank in the first place."

"The goods?" My lip twitches at the way this man talks. Like we're in an action movie or something.

"The location of the drop," he explains. "We got the time, the dock, hell, even the number of the shipping container."

"You got all that from one person." Zack's voice is low, suspicious. "Someone in the family?"

The fed picks up on it. He rolls his eyes. "Always under-estimating the law, Zack. We did our due diligence. There was a cornucopia of evidence in Frank's home office to go right alongside catching him in the act."

I remember this. The details of the arrest were explained pretty thoroughly in Zack's podcast. Though, I recall wondering why a mobster like Frank would leave so many incriminating documents out in the open. Zoe would have a field day about that.

"Who, then?" Zack leans forward, his elbows on his knees and an intense look in his eye. "Who's your infor-mant? And who's your suspect?"

Richards huffs a chuckle. "You know I can't tell you who my informant is. As far as the suspect, do you remem-ber Nick Farelli?"

Chapter Sixteen

CALM

The skin around Nick's knuckles pull taut and lose all color. My eyes are locked on them instead of my surroundings as we drive to the prison.

His face gives nothing away, but the lines of tension through his body are unmistakable.

It's a marked difference from last night when we browsed the local JcPenney for some new sheets. We both agreed that factory-fresh sheets were better than hundreds of bodies-deep sheets.

It became obvious to me that his favorite color is green. I talked him down from a more expensive set of emerald green, reminding him we would most likely be throwing them away after we leave.

The way he'd sort of pouted and reluctantly snatched the cream-colored sheets from the shelf made me press my lips together to keep from smiling.

And then we'd spent the evening remaking his bed while Karrie and TCT did... something alone in the other room—gag—and then settled in to watch a movie. An ironic twist of fate gave us a TV-edited version of Grosse Pointe Blank to watch—a mid-nineties film about a hit-man going home for his ten-year high school reunion.

We'd laughed at the blasé way the main character informs everyone what he does for a living and the comical use of blood spatter.

But that lighthearted laughter feels like the ghost of a memory in the stiff silence that fills this small car—one of his untracked back-ups. He "knows a guy" who keeps them and delivers them with supplies, as needed, no questions asked. Mob stuff, blah, blah.

This is the part where the heartwarming music swells, and I say something profound and comforting. But words don't form. How backward is that? I'm probably the smartest person in almost every situation ever, and I can't think of a single word to say.

Just pretend it's Karrie. What would I say if it were her? I'd probably make a joke about killing someone. She wouldn't think it's funny, but I certainly would. And it would distract her.

I open my mouth to try to lighten the mood, but he beats me to it.

"I need a distraction," he says through his teeth.

"Yep," I agree.

"Tell me how you got started."

I don't have to guess what he's asking me. For the first time since Karrie discovered my secret, I have someone to share my little dark pockets with. Five hundred dollars says he won't freak out about like she did, though. Definitely won't up-chuck his breakfast.

Still, I don't start talking right away.

"I know your whole thing was protecting Karrie," he adds, his body language already loosening.

Fine. I'll humor him if it means helping him relax.

"I know it's hard to believe after watching her and Tom together, but Karrie has historically had terrible taste in men."

"So you kill them?" He laughs, genuinely amused. "I'd be worried for my own neck if I didn't know I could take you."

I scoff. "I didn't kill them just because they were men. I only killed the ones who were literally the scum of the earth—the ones who hurt people or did terrible things."

"I've done a lot of terrible things," he points out, his tone mild. We might as well be talking about our favorite food.

Sushi, if you're wondering.

I give him a flat look. "For no reason? Because of the joy of it?"

His lips form a colorless line until he rubs his hand over his mouth and chin.

"You did it to protect your family, didn't you? You don't go on killing sprees or beat people up just for the hell of it."

He swallows. "No. But it colors things when I find out that family might not be worth protecting like that. I don't know Karrie that well, but I can tell she's worth keeping safe."

Well, shit, those are tears forcing their way out of my eyes. I turn to the window to gather myself before I can continue the conversation. "You do what you have to for the people who matter."

"Until you find out they're the scum of the earth." He speaks so softly, I'm not totally sure he means for me to hear.

My head swivels back in his direction. "Are we talking about the Saint?"

He shrugs, some of his tension returning. "Kids are off limits."

"Yeah, I know it's a rule."

"It's *my* rule," he interrupts, flames in his voice now. "It just happens to align with what I thought my family stood for, too. Why I did what I did for them all these years."

I pull my bottom lip between my teeth. The whole point of this conversation was to redirect his mind, but here we are. "So why roll over on the Saint? Why not just take him out?"

He's quiet for a long time, like turning into the parking lot takes some extra concentration. He might not even know how to answer me.

"Because he raised me," he finally says.

I nod as we pull into the visitor parking spot, the huge chain-link fence looming in front of us like a foreboding warning. I'm suddenly nervous for Nick, knowing that his last visit is what triggered the hit on his life.

The hit that got Stretch killed.

I grab his arm as he leans to open his door. He turns his dark, questioning eyes on me. "Do you have a disguise or something?"

He smirks. "You worried about me, Edge?"

I wrinkle my nose. "Edge?"

He mock-swings his arm like he's slicing at the air with a knife.

I snort. "I'm the nickname queen. I'm not supposed to get one."

"There's a first time for everything," he says, leaning dangerously close to me, our noses nearly brushing as he digs around behind his seat for the pack I saw him toss back there when we got in.

I'm frozen by the feeling that shoots down to my toes—like I swallowed a live wire. Or a dangerous poison. It has to be that. Someone has slipped me some kind of toxic elixir because this surely can't be normal. For me, anyway. I'd always thought I was born without the capacity for these kinds of feelings. So a sorcerer must've cast a spell on me or something.

"You got a nickname for me?" he asks as he pulls a baseball cap out, placing it over his dark hair.

I swallow, realizing I hadn't tracked the conversation because of his proximity and how sad I am to see his wavy locks tucked into the hat. So stupid. Is this what Karrie feels like every time she sees a pack of chiseled abs? I'm starting to hate that I might now understand her lack of discretion.

But getting that flustered makes me vindictive, not to mention I doubt he'd like either of his previous nicknames. "Wasn't it McMurder Pants?"

His expression darkens just slightly, but it's clearly for show. "Uh-uh. You have to come up with one yourself."

"You know," I say, zipping up my jacket, "eight out of ten guys I give nicknames to end up dead."

He reaches for his door handle. "I've already said I could take you."

I lift a brow. "The blade I had at your balls the other night would beg to differ."

His grin gets bigger before he gets out of the car, and I follow. "Don't pretend that was your original plan."

I gape at him, appalled that he knows, that there is a person capable of understanding me in that way. And damn if I'm not a little bit—what is this?—turned on?

But by the time we reach the sidewalk, his expression is flat and hard, all joking disintegrating, and those feelings I have for him turn on the impulse (or maybe some previously-forgotten instinct) to take his hand.

We walk to the door like that, and it is the weirdest sensation having a hand so warm and large engulfing mine. It's a stark contrast to Karrie's. Or maybe it's because holding her hand has never stirred that sick and elated feeling in my gut.

I'm grateful for the process of getting through sign-in and security measures for visiting hours. It keeps me distracted. We're not the only ones here, and the others are in various emotional states. Some are nervous like Nick; others seem overly resigned. And that lady—yep, she's definitely one of those who fell in love with an inmate after writing letters. One of the weird ones they talk about on those murder documentaries.

We don't wait long before the corrections officer calls everyone forward and leads us all through a heavy-duty door into a brightly-lit, if stark, hallway. I can't help the shiver that dances down my spine at how cold and unfeeling the solid concrete walls are.

I glance behind us, and it's like the door we came through shrinks before my eyes. For the first time in a long time, I feel the weight of the lives I've taken and how this could be my reality if I ever get caught.

Nick takes my hand this time, pulling my attention forward. He offers me the briefest smile that tells me he knows where my mind has gone.

He knows what I'm feeling.

I can't muster the strength to smile back, but I give his hand a squeeze as we go through a series of secured doors and cold hallways to a large room with tables evenly spaced throughout. It reminds me of a school lunchroom.

Nick picks the table at the farthest end. No doubt it's to provide us with some semblance of privacy given that it's the last one in the row, putting us next to a brick wall on one side.

He slides easily into his seat, his body going inhumanly still as I settle next to him. No one would suspect his nerves by looking at him.

I glance around the room, noting a guard standing by every door in sight—the one we came from and another that's tucked in the corner marked *emergency exit*. The final one is the door I assume leads to the inmates' section.

Indeed, within a few minutes, the door buzzes open, and people start filing in.

Frank the Saint is the fourth to come through the door, and I hardly recognize him from the pictures I've seen. His hair is shaggy, his beard is unkempt, and there are smudges of purple under each of his dark eyes as they lock onto Nick in surprise. Despite his apparent surprise, his steps don't falter as he makes his way over.

We'd been instructed to keep our hands on the tabletop, but I sense Nick's urge to pull his away as the Saint lowers his bulky frame into the chair across from us.

The Saint's eyes shift to me. "Who's your pretty friend, Nicky?"

"We're not here to talk about my friend." Nick's gravelly voice is mild, but there's an undercurrent of a threat his uncle doesn't miss.

His beard twitches with a smile. "Still unhappy with me, I see."

A tight exhale floats over Nick's lips. "I came for answers, not to hash out the past."

The Saint tips his head to the side. "Ah, my boy, I'm afraid you'll be disappointed. The two are inexorably linked."

I don't know what I expected of a man like Frank the Saint, but I certainly didn't picture him having an upper-level lexicon. Admittedly, my expectations for the intelligence of most humans is fairly dismal. Karrie thinks I'm a snob. But I consider myself a realist.

Nick ignores his uncle's comment. "Who did you teach to do your mark?"

Frank's brow lifts, and he still looks way too amused.

Before this moment, I thought some level of kindness, family loyalty, or fatherly affection would be apparent in the interaction between these two. But this man is a career criminal. One who ruled with fear and intimidation, who would order his own family murdered if it was warranted in his mind, and I want to slap the smirk off his face. Possibly with a knife.

"Now, Nicky, I need to be wooed," the Saint says. "We can't just skip the small talk and get to the nitty gritty off the bat."

"Quit fucking around," I grit through my teeth.

The Saint lets out a low whistle and winks at me. "Oooh, a feisty one. Where'd you find her, Nicky? Hooters?"

Nick's hand shoots forward in a blur of movement, and I only realize he's bending Frank's middle finger back when Frank's chair scrapes back a few inches, his expression twisted.

The closest guard spots us, but when Nick meets his eye, his face swings away.

That sends a little thrill of uncertainty down my spine. These people absolutely know who Frank is—obviously. But it's clear they know who Nick is, too. It's something I should probably remember.

"You don't talk about her or *to her* that way. You show her the respect she deserves, or I snap your fingers one by one." Nick's voice is low and dangerous, a pot of boiling oil ready to tip and burn flesh.

Frank's laugh is genuine and a little psychotic sounding, especially paired with the entrenched grimace on his face. Like the pain is hilarious to him. The Saint never seemed so ill-fitting as a nickname, even if it was meant to be ironic.

Nick releases him only once their eyes lock, and it feels too much like two alpha dogs having a showdown. I almost want to roll my eyes.

"That's the kind of loyalty I'd expect from you, Nicky." Frank laughs as he pulls his hand back, rubbing at it. "It isn't something I got, though."

"What's that supposed to mean?" Nick growls.

"Five years, Nicolas," Frank says darkly, all amusement gone from his demeanor. "How many times have you come to see me?"

Nick's hand curls into a fist. "Bullshit, Frank. You betrayed us first."

"Did I?" Frank challenges. The first true flash of anger ignites in his dark eyes. This is a deeply rooted anger, a rage so molten and dark, it's clear it's been festering for a while. Like a blacksmith's forge kept stoked over a long period of time.

"You sold out, Frank. We had a code."

Frank is nodding at every word Nick says like someone encouraging their kid taking his first steps. "We did have a code, Nicky boy. I never broke the code. I'm a lot of things, but a liar about that ain't one. I told you when I took you in that I'd never deceive you."

Nick swallows, but his sharp glare doesn't loosen.

"If you didn't, Frank, who did?" I interject. "Because your whole case was predicated on that container full of kids, and you were the one standing there when it was discovered."

Frank looks at me, a flicker of surprise dancing across his face. Then he leans forward. "Why are you asking about my mark?"

This is probably meant as his lead-in for an answer, but I find the abrupt change in direction frustrating.

Nick grinds his teeth for a moment, the debate happening in his mind shifting as he glances at me, telling me he's willing to go with it. His question pulses in the air between us. Share what we know?

I tip my head slightly. "Stretch is dead," I say, swinging my attention back to Frank. "After he warned Nick someone was out for him."

Frank strokes his chin, sitting back. Seemingly unperturbed, but that's likely a mask. "He had the mark?"

Nick nods slowly. "And I was told Vinnie went state's evidence because of your case. Turns out, his kid was killed right after you went to prison."

His brows quirk now. "With the mark."

Not a question.

Neither of us respond, knowing this is answer in itself.

Frank purses his lips. "Nicky, I was going to teach you."

Nick slaps a hand on the table. "I don't need your apology or your overdue gestures. I need a fucking answer."

A shiny edge sneaks into Frank's unflinching gaze, the chasm of hurt caused by whatever he did (or may not have done), becoming more and more clear to him. "This is a family business, Nicolas. Who do you think I'd teach?"

Chapter Seventeen

COLLECTED

My breath hitches, and I let out a little cough.

Beside me, Zack maintains his composure. Barely. His hand clenches the pen tightly, his knee bobbing until I put a hand on his thigh to steady him.

"Nick testified against Frank," Zack murmurs. "There's no way he's trying to step into his uncle's shoes."

"People change," Richards says. He stands, cracking his fingers and giving Zack an annoyed look. "Frank is guilty. It was decided by a judge and jury. Now his nephew is trying to restart the trafficking business. If we hadn't gotten the heads up from my contact, who knows when we would have figured it out."

"When?" I ask.

My voice startles both of them. Zack crooks his eyebrow. Richards frowns.

"When did this contact tell you about Nick?" I repeat.

The fed straightens his collar. Almost reluctantly, he says, "It was the day after Christmas. She called, told me

Stretch was dead, and filled me in on what Nick has been up to."

Pieces snap together in my head like a toy that is too loud at a dentist's office.

Richards' slip of the tongue seems to go unnoticed as he keeps talking to Zack. He tells him to keep an eye out, to stay away from the prison because the family has eyes on it to make sure no one gets close to Frank. He tells him they got it right all those years ago, and Zack should head back to Spokane. Richards promises to call if he gets any new information he can share.

He doesn't realize he's already shared enough. *She.* Only one name on Zoe's list was a woman. Nick's cousin. Frank's daughter. Carlotta Farelli, the woman who took over the family business when Frank was arrested.

My responses are muted, my thoughts gone from the moment as I roll the facts and figures around in my mind. The day after Christmas, Nick was gone. He couldn't have killed Stretch. Carlotta would have known that.

Stretch was found where he was killed—the blood was enough to tell. A fact I almost wish I didn't know as the hotel breakfast from this morning shifts around in my stomach at the thought. Point is, Carlotta had to be there, right? We'd thought someone had stumbled on the body. But to tell the feds where to find him she had to have seen him...

And what possible reason could she have to frame Nick unless she was doing it to protect herself?

The world around me comes into focus as Zack pushes open the thick glass door of the lobby and the two of us step onto the street. He takes my hand, tugging me down the sidewalk toward the car.

"Zack–" I begin.

"It was Carlotta," he hisses. His eyes are wide, the collected composure gone. Fear is etched across his face. "Richards said *she*."

"I know." I nod. "I was putting the pieces together. She's watching the prison. She had to see Nick go there before Christmas, thought he'd gotten some information from Frank, and decided to frame him to get him out of the way."

I pull my phone from my pocket, freezing fingers tapping quickly across the screen as I send Zoe an SOS update. Then I pull up Google and attempt a Zoe-like deep dive into everything on public record about Carlotta Farelli.

Zack slows down now that we are a few yards away from the FBI building. "Which means..."

"She probably framed Frank, too," I murmur. "That's the only thing that makes sense."

Nothing helpful comes up on the first page of searches. She's got a few appearances at large donor functions around the city. I huff a sigh of frustration, text Zoe again, and stuff my phone in my pocket.

"Kar, Nick and Zoe are at the prison right now." His voice is near-frantic.

If I wasn't also worried for our friends, it would be endearing to hear him so concerned about them.

"It'll be okay," I say, my thoughts still distracted. "Zoe's not going to let anything happen to Nick."

He pauses.

I curse under my breath. Richards isn't the only one letting things slip today.

I force out a laugh.

Zack doesn't respond in kind. He squints at me, his brow furrowed and his eyes clouded like they get when he's putting pieces of a case together in his head. A long moment passes.

"Vincent."

His murmur sends a chill through my veins. We've stopped walking now. My hands are in my pockets to keep away the cold, so he doesn't see them tighten into fists at the name.

I swallow.

He takes half a step towards me, head cocked. "Vincent," he says more firmly this time.

I give him a wide-eyed stare. "What about him?" Innocence bleeds into my tone.

"He was the only one who didn't really make sense," Zack says. He paces a few feet in front of me, one hand gripping his bag and the other running through his short hair. "He'd left town. He wasn't part of your life anymore. Even if he was coming back, how could Reginald have known that? His attention was on you. His attention was *always* on you."

I swallow again. "Zack, what are you–"

"It doesn't add up, Kar."

Heat rushes to my cheeks. Heat and panic as adrenaline floods my body, and I stare in horror as Zack keeps talking.

"Then there's Francine, the second lookalike victim," he's murmuring to himself again, not looking at me for confirmation as his pacing continues. Three steps one way, three steps back. Over and over as my life unravels like an old sweatshirt.

"She was killed that same day," he says. "I wondered how that was possible. But it wasn't overly far. He *could* have done it... He *could* have gotten back to Vincent in time... but..."

He finally whips around, facing me head-on. "Zoe did it, didn't she?"

I open and close my mouth like a drowning fish. "Zack—"

His eyes widen as every lie I've ever told him is bared in the shocking light of the truth. He takes a step back, betrayal etched across his face. "She did. She killed Vincent."

My face tells him everything.

"And more," he murmurs. "Oh shit, Karrie. Did she kill *all of them?*"

I shake my head, tears burning in my eyes and a guilt so hot it feels as though it's melting my insides. "Not all of them. Just the ones..." I inhale through my nose, clenching my teeth and hissing out a breath. I glance around, making sure we're alone.

A few people walk purposefully down the opposite street, business clothes suggesting they're on their way to work. The only motion on our side is a gray van pulling up to the curb about twenty feet away.

I take a few steps closer to the buildings, away from the street. "Just the ones who hurt people, Zack. She didn't touch any of those women, or..." I grit my teeth. "Or the men who were kind. She didn't kill Connor."

He shakes his head, twisting hurt and confusion mar his handsome face.

"Zack, I'm... I'm sorry." I put a hand on his arm, but he pulls away. "I didn't want to keep this secret from you, but I couldn't..." I swallow.

Noise disrupts my apology. The cluster of people exiting the van aren't quiet. I try to ignore them.

I meet Zack's eyes, fear and guilt slamming through me with every beat of my heart. "I didn't know about any of it until after I met you. Until we started investigating together. I had to protect her. I'm sorry."

He opens his mouth, and I don't know what is coming out. His features, usually soft and open, are impossible to read.

"Well, shit," he whispers.

I frown, confusion swamping everything else for a second. Then I track his eyeline. He's staring behind me.

I turn slowly, my eyes widening as the muzzle of a gun comes into sight. It's inches from my face, pointed directly at Zack. Another, barely a foot away, points at me.

I stumble backwards, bumping into Zack. His hands grip my upper arms, the sturdy warmth from his fingers only going so far to soothe my nerves.

The men before us are tall, white, dressed all in black, and dangerous-as-fuck looking. The thicker of the two is vaguely familiar.

Another rush of fear pushes me even closer to Zack as I note the similarity between this man and Nick. A cousin, perhaps.

"In the van," the other one says. His voice is calm. As though this is a natural occurrence for them.

Which it probably is. Kidnapping feels like it goes along with mob activity.

"Where are you taking us?" Zack asks.

I glance up at him. He gives my arms a brief squeeze.

The one who looks like Nick's cousin grins.

Fear settles cold and hard in my stomach, and at the same time I can't help the epic frustration that an actual–important–conversation with Zack is getting interrupted.

"There's someone who wants to see you."

Chapter Eighteen

AN UNDERSTANDING

Nick, Frank, and I sit in silence. Some part of me knew this must've been the answer. Knowing the kind of loyalty the Farellis are (in)famous for, it makes sense that our Prima Donna, Carlotta, would be the one he'd teach. After all, she took over when he was arrested.

But it stirs in my gut like a bad sushi roll.

Prima Donna knew the mark. She carved it into the flesh of that boy and then Stretch. I briefly entertain the morbid thoughts about what kind of implement would carve it so perfectly into something as soft and squishy as human skin, especially after they're dead.

The look of betrayal I expect doesn't show on Nick's face, but a muscle in his jaw jumps. Maybe he'd been having suspicions, too. Or maybe, like his uncle, he's very good at keeping his reactions under wraps.

Well, despite Nick's apparent calm, I feel a murderous haze creep through my mind. I want to hurt the people who have betrayed him, just like I wanted to (and did) take out the men who hurt Karrie.

"Carlotta ordered a hit on me," Nick informs his uncle.

Frank blinks slowly. There's something in his demeanor—the stillness that Nick must've inherited or actively imitated taking over. It's the clue that tells me this is how they process without showing their weakness.

But his wheels are turning just like Nick's. I've ceased to exist in their minds, which is usually my preference when there are other people.

This unspoken staring contest they've engaged in makes me antsy though, because we now have information we need to get to Tom and Karrie as soon as possible. It could be something important for Tom's FBI guy.

"Why now?" Frank finally asks. All of his smugness is gone. "What happened to trigger the hit?"

Nick's eyes flicker away briefly. "I came here. Right before Christmas. On Dad's..."

Frank's expression softens so infinitesimally, I might've missed it if I hadn't been studying the micro changes in Nick's face every time a new emotion floods him. Those minute shifts have trained me to recognize it in his uncle's expression.

It suddenly clicks with the timing, and I picture a little orphaned Nick being taken in right around Christmas after his dad died. I picture Frank and Carlotta rushing to get extra presents to stick under the tree for a little lost kid whose dad had been emotionally gone many years before he was physically gone.

"You didn't come in," Frank says.

"But someone thought I did."

Their eyes become slits at the same moment, and it's like looking at a man staring at himself in the mirror.

"The question is why would Carlotta be worried about Nick coming here?" I ask, though the answer is fairly obvious as I stare hard at Frank.

He runs his tongue along his teeth, and there's a lot less surprise in his body language than I feel there should be, confirming my suspicions.

"How long have you suspected her of framing you?" My question comes out flat, and it lands hard.

"You pick up fancy college girls now, Nicky?" Frank asks him with a wry twist to his mouth.

"You *didn't* break the code, did you?" I insist, not letting Nick respond to the stupid jab.

Nick turns to me, eyes wide, but I keep my focus solely on Frank.

"You knew *someone* framed you. But you didn't know who." I shake my head while both men stare at me. It feels more like I'm having a conversation with myself for all the response I get from them. "But you started to suspect. Because it had to be someone close to you, someone who knew all the ins and outs *and* how to hide stuff from you."

When Frank glances at Nick from the corner of his eye, another little piece falls into place in my mind.

"You thought it was Nick." That explains why he was poking the bear so much when we got here, trying to get a rise out of his nephew. It was pitiful, but it was he was left with for revenge. "But the mark gave it away."

Nick swallows, his adam's apple bobbing with the force. "Carlotta betrayed you. And she let me believe it was you, let me carry on while she was running the whole fucking operation."

I put my hand on his arm before he has a chance to shove the chair back. I can feel the heat of his anger at the fresh treachery through our touch. "She ordered the hit because she thought you came in to see her dad and found something out. She thought you would come for her."

"She's right about one thing," Nick says through his teeth. "I won't let this slide. Not this kind of betrayal of my trust, of Frank's trust, of the family's code."

"Nicky, don't be rash." There's very real panic in Frank's voice, and it's hard for me to reconcile that level of protection for the daughter who let *him* go down for something she had done. "She's family."

Nick is vibrating with fury, and based on Frank's behavior, Nick angry is both rare and worrisome.

"We have to tell Karrie and Tom. He needs to let his FBI guy know, so they can take Carlotta in." I'm staring at Nick, at the glinting rage as it morphs like molten lava changing the landscape around it. "We will make sure she pays for her crimes."

My voice lands hard on the words to underscore my true meaning: we're not going to kill her for Frank's sake, for the sake of Nick's relationship with the man who took him in and raised him.

His jaw ticks, but Nick nods his agreement. "I'm going to make this right, Frank."

"I'm sorry, Nicky," is all Frank says as we stand.

Visiting time isn't quite over, but the urgency of this information keeps us from staying put any longer. Now that the truth is about to come out, though, I know Nick will be back again to rebuild what had been demolished five years before. This revelation might have destroyed a piece of his family, but it restored a bigger one.

A guard steps forward to take us from the room, his bushy brows rising toward his hairline, but he doesn't ask why we're cutting our visit short.

We go back through the long hallway that sends shivers skating along my spine for a different reason this time. My fingers itch to get my phone to check in with Karrie to see how their meeting went and to plan our next steps.

The discomfort and uncertainty crawls through my bones, and I can feel the heat of Nick's anger still rolling off of him in waves. It makes the urgency rise inside my chest as we emerge back into what I can only inaccurately describe as a lobby.

The sun has miraculously made an appearance, and it cuts in through the windows, stinging my eyes after all the artificial light in the hallway and the visitor area.

It strangely amps my nerves up, and dread wends its way around my limbs as we trudge toward the guard who took our things before we were brought back to Frank. I can't help snatching my purse from the woman's hand and digging immediately for my hand sanitizer before I even touch my phone—despite my eagerness to text Karrie.

If we can catch them at their meeting, maybe we can get the ball rolling on Carlotta—handling it the legal way instead of resorting to Nick's (and my) less savory tactics. But only for Frank's sake. Because, in a roundabout way, it's for Nick's sake, too.

"Service sucks in here," I mutter, handing the sanitizer to Nick without being asked.

He smiles gratefully as he takes it and spins to lead the way toward the doors.

"Place gives me the creeps," he growls as we emerge into the crisp air that bites at my skin despite the rare winter sunshine.

I hum my agreement as the service bars slowly illuminate on my phone, kicking my heartbeat up several notches as they do.

Before I can even open my text app, a message pops up on my screen from Karrie, and my heart stutters because the first thing I see is "SOS."

My hand shoots out to clutch at Nick's jacket sleeve, yanking him to a stop. His eyes are intense as his thick brows crash together.

"They know it was Carlotta."

"That makes things easier," he murmurs, the sound rumbling.

I nod and tap on the screen, flipping through the options to call her instead of texting back. This is all too time-sensitive to type back and forth.

I begin walking toward the car again as I press the phone to my ear with a weird knot forming in my stomach. It gets tighter as the call goes straight to voicemail.

Pulling the phone away to retry the call, I glare at the screen, aware of the swiftness with which Nick buckles himself in and starts the car, whipping out of his parking space.

I buckle as I bring the phone to my ear again, once more getting Karrie's chipper voicemail greeting.

I don't like it.

I try Tom next, the air in my lungs growing thicker.

The sound of my breathing draws Nick's attention. "What's wrong?" he asks as I lower my phone.

"Neither of them are answering."

"Still in their meeting?" He flips a turn signal, a determined set to his expression.

"I don't think it would automatically go to voicemail."

He shoots me a skeptical look.

"They'd ignore the calls, but it would ring first. Karrie *never* turns her phone off." Not since I made her swear not to after Vincent. It took a few of my scoldings to get her to officially agree, but it's been years since she's done anything but restart the thing. It's also been years that I've had the tracking app on her phone linked to mine. She has no idea it's even there.

When I pull that up, it doesn't show a live location or movement. Just a check-in for last known location.

Nick rolls his lips inward as he thinks and drives.

"Do you know the area around West Seattle Bridge?"

His scowl deepens. "Oh, yes. We have a building out there for..." He doesn't stop himself abruptly, but the heavy implication is still obvious. More of that mafia training to be careful what you say because he's not trailing off for my nonexistent delicate sensibilities.

"Prima Donna was watching the prison before," I muse. "I bet she's got eyes on it at all times."

He meets my gaze.

"I'm guessing she knows we were there."

Almost as soon as I finish the thought, the noisy rattle of his phone vibrating in the cupholder snatches our attention, and he pulls into the nearest empty spot along the street parking. The meter blinks that it needs payment, but he doesn't turn off the engine as he picks up his phone.

A glint of rage flashes in his eyes as they lock on mine. He hits speakerphone when he answers. "Carlotta."

There's no mistaking the entire conversation he poured into that one word.

"Nicky," she says, and I can hear her smile. "How the hell are you?" There's also a knife in that tone.

"It doesn't matter how I am. What does matter is how you're going to feel when I get my hands on you."

She tsks. "That's cute." All pretense of cheer is gone, and there's a threat humming through her words. "Here's how this is going to go: you're going to march your ass to FBI headquarters to turn yourself in to Agent Doug Richards. Because obviously you're going down for Stretch and for the work you did trying to keep up Dad's newer endeavors."

"You bitch. Your own father?" Nick gives his head a tight shake. "What kind of loyalty is that? It's not the Farelli family I knew."

She laughs. "Oh, Nicky. My baby cousin with the moral code. Things change."

"I'm not going down for this."

"Oh, you will," she purrs. "You will do what I say or your friends get intimately acquainted with my new enforcers. They don't have the same code you do."

Nick's eyes widen as he looks at me. I slap a hand over my mouth before my panic can shove words out.

"Why, Lottie?" he growls.

She laughs again, the sound sending a cascade of chills down my spine. "Don't ask stupid questions, Nicky. You have thirty minutes."

She hangs up, and Nick stares down at the screen as if it were a door she'd slammed in his face.

"Shit," he says once he recovers. And then he throws the car into drive and guns it out of the parking space, whipping around to head the opposite direction.

"You're not turning yourself in," I say, clutching the center console for stability.

He shakes his head, both hands gripping the wheel. "We're getting Zack and Karrie out of that warehouse and taking Carlotta the fuck down."

CHAPTER NINETEEN

SNITCHES GET SNATCHED

The black hood placed over my head does exactly nothing to stop me hearing every single thing around us. There's just an annoying scratchy overtone to it all.

Zack is beside me still, his arms bound behind his back the same way mine are. I assume he wears a matching hood, but I can't see shit.

Two of the men who snatched us ride up front. One is in the back, his outline barely visible through the fabric across my face when the light hits just right. They're relatively quiet. I only pick up a discussion about where to get dinner, an argument about the radio, and a single phone call to confirm capture.

The guy who called Carlotta has his volume on loud. Her voice, deeper than I'd expected and hazy like a smoker's, is soft and deadly, sending a shudder down my spine.

Zack feels it. We're pressed close together. I can feel his bouncing leg.

"Hey," he murmurs. "It's gonna be okay."

I swallow back a hysterical chuckle. "Okay? How is it going to be okay?"

He hesitates but leans into me a little more. "Well, we've got two friends who are capable of just about anything."

"Unless they get captured, too," I say weakly. Tears well in my eyes. When they fall, they soak into the nasty smelling cloth hood. "That's why I never told you..." My emotions, already so close to the surface with everything going on, bubble over. "I just wanted to keep her safe, Zack. I never wanted to lie to you. I never wanted to keep the truth from you."

My voice gets louder, but I couldn't care less what these mobsters think about my mental breakdown.

"At first it was to keep you safe," I continue, my voice thick with tears. "I didn't know how far she'd go. But then Connor happened, and I found out the truth. And Reginald took you, and we tracked him down, and he was such a *sick asshole*." I sniff, unable to wipe the snot from my nose as I try to breathe slowly enough to not hyperventilate. "The world is a better place with him gone, and that—him taking you—that was what finally made me see it from Zoe's perspective. I'd do anything for her. For you."

I break off, a sob cutting through my words.

"But you didn't trust me enough to tell me," Zack says, his voice as quiet as it had been before.

The van takes a sharp left. At the front, someone turns off the music and puts on coverage of a Seahawks game.

I hang my head, feeling myself pull away from him even though I only want to press closer to his warmth. "I didn't know how you'd react. And then, so much time had passed... I know that's why." I break down in another wave of tears.

"What?" He sounds genuinely confused.

"I know that's why you don't want to marry me," I sob. "Because some part of you, that detective spidey sense you have knew I was keeping something."

I can't keep talking. The fear and pain and tension of the last year and a half—being targeted by a serial killer, finding out my best friend is a serial killer, falling in love, hiding this damn secret, and getting pulled into another violent criminal's life...

I cry. I just sit, shoulders aching from having them pinned behind me with thick cords of rope, and cry. My face is going to look abysmal when this hood comes off. Waterproof mascara can only do so much.

Maybe ten seconds after my true melt-down happens, I feel Zack's arm wind around me.

I'm startled out of my sobs.

He doesn't try to untie me. Instead, he pulls me into him, letting my head rest on his shoulder as he strokes my arm. With his other hand, he gently tugs the hood off of my head. He uses the fabric to wipe the snot and tears from my face.

"How'd you do that?" I mumble with a sniff.

"Nick taught me a few tricks when we first met. And, for the record, you not telling me about Zoe is *not* why I haven't answered you yet."

"Then—"

"Hey!" I'm interrupted by a gruff cry from the man sitting in the back of the van with us, who finally turned around from discussing the game with the driver and shotgun passenger.

He does a crouched run across the rocking floor towards us. His breath suggests he had a garlic beef Chinese dish for lunch. I wince as rough hands grab my shoulders and shove me aside.

The van swerves at just the wrong time, and I go crashing off the bench. With my hands still behind me, my bare face slams into the floor. I yelp, and immediately the warmth of blood begins to gush from my nose.

There's a slam. I roll, glancing up in time to see Zack shaking out his fist as the mob thug clutches his jaw.

Zack swings again, but his hand is blocked with a gun. The metal bangs into his wrist. Zack hisses, wheeling backward and clutching his arm.

"Up," the mobster growls.

I shift to my knees. My face is on fire, shoulder smarting, and blood still dripping. It hits my sweater, little darker dots staining the black.

With the gun still pointed at Zack, the guy hooks a hand under my arm and yanks me upright—well, as upright as possible in the back of a moving van.

He shoves me back into Zack's arms. I glance down, taking in Zack's already swelling wrist.

"Are you okay?" I whisper.

He doesn't answer, just clutches me to him as we sink back onto the rickety bench bolted to the floor.

"Don't fucking move." The man across from us sucks in heavy breaths. He leans toward the gap to the front, not taking his eyes off us. "We close?"

The driver grunts in the affirmative.

I exhale a shaky breath.

"What's a matter, Donnie? You need help back there?" The shotgun passenger laughs to punctuate his question.

"Fuck off."

I almost laugh. Almost.

The ridiculousness of this hits me as the sharp pains ease into dull throbbing. A week ago, we were at Christmas dinner. A week ago, I thought I was about to be engaged.

"Why?" I turn my head, making as much eye contact with Zack as I'm able.

He sighs, understanding me immediately in that way he does that gives me butterflies. "I have some things to tell you before you make a commitment like that with me."

My brow furrows.

Zoe did the research. Well before Zack and I *actually* started dating. Hell, she told me his deep dark secret—a young marriage and quick divorce—the night we all almost got murdered and Zack ended up in the hospital.

My bestie may overlook some things: emotions, human contact, legal restrictions on juvie records, but she's obsessively dedicated to research. Especially when it comes to men in my life.

"Zack," I say, my voice steadier than it's been since we went to talk to the fed. "I know you were married. I know you had a young divorce. It's okay. That doesn't bother me at all."

"How do you—" he breaks off with a sigh. "Zoe."

"Yep."

"Enough," barks the man still pointing his gun at us. "We're here."

Sure enough, the van slows to a stop. The crusty bag goes roughly back over my head. I catch the sound of Zack grunting—likely his hands getting tied back behind him.

The van door slides open. We're shoved out and marched through the sun for a moment before entering some kind of building. An empty one. Big, given the echoes from my thunking boots.

I almost keep walking, but a hand grabs my arm and hauls me to a stop. I stumble. Then the arm presses me down. I sink onto what feels like a metal fold-out chair.

There is movement behind me, someone untying and retying my binds.

I'm quiet, focusing on my breathing and trying not to fall back into panic.

A moment later, the hood is pulled off again. I blow a bit of hair out of my face. My claw clip is fantastic, but it can only do so much when faced with kidnapping and multiple hoods shoved over my head.

I was wrong. Not quite empty.

This warehouse is vast. Dusty skylights in the ceiling let the only light in. It's a good twenty feet high, rusted looking steel beams barely holding the roof up.

Half-empty metal shelves sit in sporadic rows. The empty spaces build anxiety in my chest. The concrete floor has stains, and my stomach churns at the thought that some of these dark brown smudges are probably blood.

Behind me, the asshole from the van grunts, "Try getting out of those, and you'll be eating a bullet."

A flicker of relief spasms through me. I wait until the sound of the man's boots on the ground fade away.

"Zack?" I whisper.

"I'm here," he says, his voice equally quiet. "Are you okay?"

"Not particularly." I give a weak chuckle. A tear slips from the corner of my eye. "I really didn't think we'd die on this trip."

He heaves a sigh, taking my words for what they are—not a joke. "We aren't going to die, Kar."

I sniff, biting back a fresh wave of tears. "How can you know that? We know what these people do to loose ends."

He lets out a sardonic laugh. "Because Nick and Zoe are still out there."

I don't say anything, the hopelessness of the situation eating away at my insides.

"Did you hear me, Kar?" Zack says it louder this time.

I nod, realize he can't see me, and murmur a yes.

"Zoe is out there. And someone kidnapped you. What do you think she's gonna do when she finds out?"

My tears dry up as my eyes widen. "Oh yeah," I mutter.

"Yeah." He laughs again. "It's gonna get bloody in here."

I hiccup in place of a laugh. The thought of my knife wielding friend storming in and taking on a bunch of dudes with guns only stirs more fear in my stomach. "I wish we could've stayed in Texas for the holidays."

He sighs, a sad sound, not an exasperated one. "I'm so sorry, Kar."

I shake my head with a sniff. "If you hadn't left when you did, Nick would be dead. You did the right thing, I just–"

"I wanna marry you," Zack murmurs, so quiet I almost don't hear him.

I freeze, heart thudding in my chest. "What?" I whisper, afraid I heard wrong.

"I wanna marry you," he repeats. "I'm sorry it took so long to say it, Kar."

My lips twist to the side to keep more tears from falling. "You're just saying that because we're gonna die."

"No," he says it loudly. Almost loud enough to block the sound of footsteps.

Our conversation halts. The tell-tale echo of stiletto heels on concrete announces a new body to the mix. A sickly sweet, husky voice says, "Trouble in paradise?"

CHAPTER TWENTY

FLIRTING WITH DANGER

This warehouse district is such a classic scene for mob theatrics, I almost laugh. Except I'm thinking way too much about what Carlotta's guys could be doing to my best friend to see humor in much.

Instead, my brain is working through angles of evisceration before I realize I don't have any of my favorite knives.

"Weapons," I say without preamble, drawing Nick's attention.

"I have weapons," he replies, brows furrowing.

I can't help smirking. "What kinds of weapons?"

His matching grin twinkles. "All kinds."

He's not joking. When we pull around the back of one of the numerous indistinguishable buildings and get out of the car, he walks to the trunk and opens it for my eyes to dance from one option to another.

"These are guns," I point out.

Nick says nothing, one side of his mouth tilting up as he pops a compartment open, revealing a stunning selection of knives that almost makes me salivate. Which would actually be crazy. I'm *not* crazy, but I do appreciate sharp implements. Call me an enthusiast.

I select a shiny blade that winks in the sunlight that's still blazing like it's on our side. It does give me an odd shot of confidence.

"Take a couple. This might get dangerous." Nick starts loading up as he says this, and I reach for a couple more blades to stash on my person.

I still pause for brief moments of adoration. "So pretty."

"I love the way your eyes light up when you talk about knives."

"I love that you have so many knives." I lift a brow, and his smile grows. Is this flirting? Am I, Zoe Turner, flirting with a *man*? If only Karrie was here to analyze with me, even if it would mean her unending teasing that I do, indeed, have feelings. As in, more than one.

As in, I feel a whole mess of stuff inside my body as I watch Nick check the magazines in the handguns he chooses. He also manages to stuff a small package of hand wipes into his pocket amid the various firearms he stashes around his body.

And a new swirling of *feelings* tangles up inside of me.

I really need to go eviscerate someone. Maybe murdering someone will kill these feelings because they are out of control.

Suddenly, my body is alight with nerves that aren't normal for me before going in against someone. It's this electricity bouncing between us. And maybe also the fact that we're going in against people who are already armed. I don't typically put myself in a position to *get* killed. Because I'm not reckless.

I glance at Nick. He's not reckless either, but he is definitely more familiar with this kind of scenario. I might just let him take lead, though that feels so foreign even in my thoughts. Like an ill-fitted dress or that time I wore Karrie's combat boots to take out the trash. I don't usually rely on anyone else for anything, except for Karrie when it comes to grocery shopping the random items that are out of stock when I do delivery.

Nick moves amid shadows, clinging close to the wall of the nearest building. Matching his movements and pace, I keep myself close behind, stepping lightly on my toes to soften my footsteps.

Sending my mind and body back to that moment again to when I was stalking Mac in the darkness around the apartment, I figure this is more or less the same thing. Or at least offers a familiarity that calms my mind enough to focus on the fact that there are two bodies—living ones—loitering around the back door of the building across from us.

I point instead of asking, and Nick nods in confirmation, understanding it as easily as if I'd said it. Okay, another swirl in my gut.

Stop it, attraction. I don't have time for your ooey gooey bullshit.

Nick gestures to his left, and I follow his indicated path, working my way around our building to get around and behind where the two goons stand guard. If you could call it that. Their stance is so relaxed, it's clear they don't think anyone is coming for them.

They don't realize I keep my best friend on a location tracker like the overprotective cyber hacker that I am.

I spot Nick lurking in the shadows, coming from the opposite direction, creeping toward the two men who are discussing the salami sub from two different delis.

"Nah, the sides are better from Louie's," one says, arms crossed over a barrel chest. "More choices, and his slaw is to die for."

"But the bread there is always stale," his companion replies, flipping a knife out of its casing—a pretty sizeable switch-blade that he folds back in. Then he does the whole routine again.

My eyes track the movements, timing my steps with the way he does it over and over until Nick and I are close enough that I can see him mouth, "Distract them."

I take a breath, gearing up for Damsel in Distress. Don't think Seductress will work on these guys. I'm doubtful much of anything will. This area doesn't exactly lend itself to someone getting lost and then getting out of their car to seek help. But I'd rather do Damsel, and all we need is a quick window.

Nick knows what he's doing.

I stumble out of the shadows, and both men jerk to attention.

"Oh my gosh!" I say breathlessly, letting my chest heave with feigned emotion. The movement, predictably, draws their eyes. "I'm so glad you're here. My car died, and I'm so lost." I add a little giggle, internally cringing.

They both step forward, definitely on alert.

"Where's your car?" the knife flicker asks, holding the folded-in blade aloft, though his eyes have softened.

Barrel Chest is looking around behind me for a threat back there, suspicious that this is exactly what it is. But he's looking the wrong direction, and Nick slides in behind him. With a mask of intense calm, Nick slashes him across the throat with the only knife he took from his stash, moving on to the second guy before he can flip his knife back out or grab the gun I see holstered inside his blazer. In one fluid motion, Nick dispatches him the same way.

The bodies slump to the ground, and I'm amazed that there's not a drop of blood on Nick other than his shoes. Which are wrapped in those little booties he brought. When the hell did he have time to put those on?

I'm about to ask, but he speaks before I can.

"That one was my cousin, Jimmy." He's staring down at the guy who'd held the knife.

I look down, too. "Well, I suppose it was bound to happen. You have a lot of cousins."

He lifts his head to meet my gaze, his expression unreadable. Then he huffs a laugh. "Still gotta be the one who knows the most in a room."

The corner of my mouth hitches up. "We're outside."

He shakes his head, grinning, as he pulls out a wipe and uses it on his hands and the knife he holds. I'm reading his tension now. On the other side of the door that stands behind him is the cousin he trusted with his life and loyalty. And now she's the one who framed her own father for her crimes, ordered Nick's execution, and kidnapped our friends.

His hands are steady as they work, and his expression is as stoic as always. But even I know I would struggle with this kind of double-crossing.

"Ready?" he asks, tucking the knife away now that he's satisfied with its cleanliness.

"As always."

His chin dips in acknowledgement, and he leads the way to the door, slipping it open only wide enough to slide in sideways. Darkness wraps around us the second we're inside, though I can see light filtering in through windows set at intervals in the ceiling.

Nick pulls me against the wall into the shadows, flattening himself against the concrete wall and sliding to our right where we've caught movement. Maybe he missed his calling as a secret agent.

There are large racks and stacks of shelves like this is a place to store inventory. Random items lay on the shelves, and I wonder if maybe it's to throw off anyone who might be investigating. I highly doubt the Farelli family uses it for anything other than what it's being used for right now.

As we get closer to where the sounds and sight of movement drew us, a woman's voice carries back, though I can't make out what she's saying. It's a husky sound, hinting at age and maybe a disregard for the research on the detriments of smoking cigarettes.

I'd bet my best set of knives it's our Prima Donna.

CHAPTER TWENTY-ONE

WEDDING PLANS

Carlotta Farelli stalks towards us like a damn runway model. Tall, with jet black hair and a fitted gray pantsuit trimmed in black.

I'm struck by how much Nick's cousin looks like him as she strides towards us. Her smile is like a wicked version of the way Nick looks at Zoe. With him, it's admiration and affection. And, while the similarity is obvious, Carlotta looks more like a lion who has found a wounded wildebeest.

She comes to a stop in front of me, head tilted ever so slightly as she plants her hands on her hips. "Everything okay with the lovebirds?"

I glare up at her, chest still heaving from Zack's words—as skeptical as I am about his sudden acceptance of my proposal. "Eat shit, lady. We aren't telling you anything."

"Oh." She chuckles. "You don't have to *tell* me anything. You aren't here for whatever limited information you might have. You're hostages."

My throat closes briefly. I've watched enough crime TV to know what happens to a hostage when the kidnapper gets what they want. My breath comes too quick, and I fear hyperventilation is on the near horizon.

"Kar," Zack's voice is soft, but loud enough for me to hear even though he's behind me. His fingers find mine, and I find relief in the fact that he is so close. "I want to spend the rest of my life with you. I love you, and I'm sorry I didn't just sit down and talk to you about it."

Carlotta's brow furrows, her lips pinching as she darts a glance at him before looking back at me. "Your boyfriend here almost caused me a world of problems a few years ago." She takes a step to the side, barely visible in my peripheral vision as she addresses Zack. "You were so close to figuring it all out. Not bad for an amateur detective."

I snarl, anger cutting through my panic. "He's a fucking fantastic detective, bitch."

She grins, and then Zack speaks again. Still to me. He's completely ignoring her.

"I'm thinking a beach wedding," he says, his voice louder this time. "Black on black tux, you in black lace."

I huff a laugh as Carlotta scoffs.

Her voice, sharp now, no longer sticky sweet, cuts across the sound. "You're not going to have a wedding. My cousin is going to turn himself in. If he's lucky, he'll get maximum security and solitary confinement. If not—"

"You think lace on the beach is a good look?" I interrupt. My throat is still thick, my words a bit choked. But I push through the fear and tears. Zack's calloused fingers help pull me through the darkness.

He chuckles, the sound echoing through the vast space. Beside me, I can practically feel Carlotta seething.

"I think you can pull it off," he says. "You make black look good everywhere. You're gonna need full length sleeves though, or you'll burn like a lobster."

I laugh again.

"Enough," Carlotta snaps.

She stalks back around, planting her hands on the armrests of the chair and staring me in the eye. The scent of her nail polish—usually a smell I enjoy—stings my nostrils.

"This isn't a fucking vacation weekend. You two are going to be dead as soon as the call comes in."

I meet her gaze.

I think about this evil bitch's plan. To get Nick arrested for a murder he didn't commit. To kill me and Zack. To kill Zoe. To keep running the Farelli family business—a business that involves trafficking kids. I think about how dangerous it is to get under her skin. And I process how much I want to piss her off before Zack and I die. The edges of my mouth slide up in a smirk.

"What else held up the answer?" I ask.

She frowns at me and opens her mouth. I speak before she gets a word out.

"Not you. Zack? There was the divorce, but what else stopped you from answering?"

The bitch's face goes cherry red. I don't think I've seen someone this mad since the day Zoe found out Vincent hit me.

Her fingers dig into the armrests, knuckles going white. The chair makes an audible groan. Around us, the goons exchange nervous glances.

Zack's fingers brush against mine. A back and forth motion like when I tickle his shoulders with my long nails to ease his anxiety during a rough case.

"Is now the time?" he asks, his voice a little shaky.

Carlotta scoffs. "No," she snarls, her rough voice breaking across her words. "It's not the fucking time."

"Yeah," I cut across her again. The woman's head might explode if she keeps getting redder. "I want to know what was keeping us apart, Zack."

I can almost picture the nod he does to hype himself into saying something he's scared to say. His fingers tremble.

"I can't have kids, Kar."

Even Carlotta looks surprised by this. She opens and then closes her mouth. Her grip on the chair loosens a bit.

I blink a few times, my brow furrowed as I wrack my brain for any instance of me even suggesting we have kids. Ever.

Nothing. I search internally for a hint of disappointment at his words, a stirring of anything in my heart that might make me hesitate. Nothing.

"I don't..." I let out a nervous chuckle. "I don't want kids, babe. I've never wanted kids. Not after what I went through. I figured you'd feel the same way."

There is silence. An odd, dead silence in this echoey room that catches every sound. Carlotta wrinkles her face, the make-up around her eyes creasing.

From behind me, I hear Zack catch his breath with a soft sob. "I thought you might... it's why it didn't work out with my ex. She really wanted kids, and we didn't know until..."

"I don't," I repeat firmly. "I don't want kids, Zack. I want *you*. I want us to get married on the beach in black on black and lace. I want to torture Zoe by kissing the hell out of you every New Year's Eve. I want to spend our mornings cleaning so those germaphobe assassins come over for brunch. I want to—"

"That's *enough*." Carlotta's low voice is disturbingly scarier than her loud one. She tilts her head at me, a crazy haze over her eyes. "What part of *you're about to die*, do you not understand?"

"What part of *our friends are murderers*, do *you* not understand?" I snap back. "You fucked up betraying your family because it was a fucked up thing to do. But this?" I jerk against my restraints, looking around the warehouse with pointed incredulity. "Kidnapping the besties of people ready to bleed the world to protect us? Dumb. Fucking. Move."

Her hand moves so fast I don't have time to flinch. She strikes me across the face, her nails digging into my skin. Heat flashes, my cheek throbbing, blood trickling down to my jawline.

"*Oh hell no,*" a very familiar voice shouts from a space I can't see.

I scrunch up my face to try and shake away some of the sting. Footsteps thud against the ground. Someone running. There is a thunk, a familiar squelch of a knife plunged into someone's flesh. Metallic tasting saliva warns me of my distaste for gore.

Carlotta dances back from my chair, her eyes wide with alarm as a blade spins through the air toward her. It lodges into her shoulder, and she lets out a piercing screech. Blood oozes down her shirt.

I gag. Then a flash of blonde distracts from my upset tummy.

I shake my head, still holding down vomit, and mumble, "Told ya so."

MOB CLEAN-UP IN AISLE TWO

Rage is a fire in my blood so hot that I can barely feel my hands as I slash my second knife into another goon as he turns to block my way to Prima Donna. It slides so easily in and out of his neck that I praise Nick's "guy" for providing the very top quality steel.

I reposition my now-bloody knife, all without breaking stride, and the fury flares as Prima Donna looks at me with equal parts incredulity and animosity. When I bring my weapon in a sweeping arc toward her, she blocks me, knocking it from my hands like she doesn't already have my first blade in her designer-clad shoulder.

Because, of course. She's a damn mob boss with violence and death as a staircase to her throne.

I start to come back to myself, distantly noting that Nick is taking care of the final two goons Prima Donna had with her when she assaulted my best friend.

The thought alone threatens to light me on fire again, and I feel inside my jacket for the last knife I have stashed. I should at least subdue the Prima Donna but leave her for Nick—this *is* supposed to be his showdown.

But I'm surprised again by how spry she is. She might be at least a decade older than Nick, but she's *fit*. Her smoker's voice was misleading, and I'm a little annoyed and awed to find she spins away from me easily, pulling a gun and firing off a couple rounds as she dives for a row of shelves nearby.

I drop to the concrete and roll toward Karrie and Tom. I need to get them as low to the ground as possible now that Prima Donna has her weapon *and* cover. I shift to analyze their bindings and grope along the floor for the knife I'd dropped, my eyes catching on Nick as he straightens. There's a limp goon on the floor at his feet, blood pooling around his bootie-covered shoes.

I flick my head in the direction his cousin went, and he nods, pulling a gun from some hidden place on his body.

"It's so freaky how in sync you guys are," Karrie says, huffing breathlessly. Her eyes are huge from fear. Understandable, given that stray bullets went flying past her head a moment ago.

Using the recovered blade, I slice through her bindings and turn my attention to Tom's immediately upon her release.

The explosive sound of another gunshot pierces the air, and Tom, Karrie, and I dive for the cold concrete floor. Karrie immediately starts retching, and it reminds me of Mac when he's hacking up a hairball—unpleasant and inconveniently timed.

"Watch it, Nicky!" Prima Donna calls out. She's moving between rows of shelving, but I can see that Nick is tracking the sound of her voice.

"All I want to do is talk, Lottie," he answers, the rumble of his voice loud enough to carry without much effort.

No one in this room believes he just wants to talk.

"Alright, Nicky. Let's talk." She's moving again.

I urge Tom and Karrie toward the door we came in to get them out of sight and away from the line of fire and the dead bodies. Karrie's still gagging.

"Let's start with the whore you're putting above your family."

I ignore the jab and focus my attention on Karrie's pale visage.

"Keep that vomit locked up, Kar. Your stomach contents will connect us with a very big and very messy crime scene."

Karrie shuts her eyes at my warning and sucks a breath in through her nose.

"First of all," Nick says, his voice reverberating through the room. Frankly, it's disorienting, and I realize he's probably used this space for murdery deeds more than she has. "She's no whore. Second of all, you put your own dad in prison."

There's a pause, and I shove Karrie and Tom around the corner before turning to see what's happening behind me.

Nick is slinking around a shelf, his gun held up by his face in a classic pose.

Then there's a flurry of motion as he lurches forward, jutting a leg out, and the Prima Donna screeches as she sails to the floor, her gun skittering away from her. She flips as soon as she hits, and Nick's heavy shoe lands on her hand and keeps her from moving.

He raises the gun to her face.

"Third," he drawls, his voice more deadly than the gun he's holding, "this isn't my family anymore." The flash of the muzzle startles me more than the sound of him firing does.

Even after his cousin goes still, Nick stares down at her for a long beat.

I motion for Tom and Karrie to stay put, then get to my feet, checking my surroundings to be sure no one else might be lurking and walk toward him.

His breathing is even, his face impassive, but he continues to stare. I reach into his pocket for the wipes and pull a couple out for him. He takes them from me without moving any other muscle.

Is he searching for the remorse inside himself, like I sometimes do? Or is this his way of mourning this double loss—the loss of who he thought she was and her life?

After a moment, he puts his gun away and finishes wiping his hands thoroughly, then he finally looks at me. There's an unspoken question in his eyes.

"They're safe." I tip my head to where Karrie and Tom are hiding.

He nods, then takes a chance, hesitating only a fraction before he touches my face. "You good?"

I offer a small grin. "I'm fine. Karrie's ready to upchuck her breakfast, though. And I'm guessing we should probably clear out as soon as possible."

His eyes narrow as he looks around. "I need to send a message."

I cock my head to the side. "What kind of message?"

He didn't mean a literal message.

We pile up all the bodies—and by "we," I mean, Nick and myself because Karrie would *never* and Tom's sense of right and wrong is not as fluid as literally all the rest of us. Then Nick douses them in the lighter fluid and gasoline cans that are conveniently available to us.

The fact that he knew where they were and why there's such an abundance in the first place tells me this is very on-brand for him, even though it feels mob-movie epic and cool as shit.

I'm losing my mind a little bit with how into him I am feeling after this whole fiasco.

He tosses his little booties from earlier onto the pile (we donned fresh pairs he brought as extras), along with the plethora of wipes he's used throughout the process.

Dragging a match along the friction strip of the box, a flame flares to life in his hand. He flicks it at the pile in the center, and it's a little show just for us, since Kar and Tom are sitting in Nick's car, pretending nothing is going on here. It's like a romantic (and morbid) fireworks display.

"The bodies will stay intact unless that fire reaches 1500 degrees fahrenheit," I inform him.

He laughs. "Good thing I'm not looking to burn them completely."

I blink, realization settling. "This is the message?"

He shrugs, his eyes on the line of flames running between the bodies, growing as it consumes the chemical-covered flesh. "This means it's done. And those in the family will know it. The feds will, too."

He takes my hand and tugs me toward the door.

"And what about the Saint?"

Nick's mouth compresses. "I know where Carlotta keeps her files. Problem is," he says, pausing to open the door and let me go first, "they got him on a lot of other stuff. I can only get the trafficking rap off him."

I can hear the faint disappointment in his tone, sensing the layers in it. He's disappointed about more than one thing, but my inability to understand normal human emotions prevents me from making the connection initially.

"Wait, so the family is—"

"It's done," he interrupts, his car coming into view.

I can just barely make out the shape and movement of people in the back seat, and a little spike of panic in my blood sharpens my thoughts. What if we missed someone? But then the backdoor flings open, and a long fishnet-clad leg shoots out.

I stop Nick and turn him to face me. "The family is done?"

"There's no one to take over." He shrugs.

I lift my brows, and it elicits his soft smile.

"I never wanted to be in charge." He bends to take off his fresh pair of booties.

When he's done, I grip his shoulder to remove my own. "Isn't that against traditional practice or something? Always have someone in the wings to take over?"

His mouth twists wryly. "I thought you knew everything, Edge."

I huff. "Alright, *McMurder Pants*, I didn't do research on the hierarchical structure of the Italian mafia. But if the Farelli crime family is no more, what are you going to do?"

There's a little twinkle in his dark eyes. "The Armchair Detective could use a colorful co-host, don't you think?"

"Are you guys done?" Karrie's tight voice cuts through my focus, so I'm unable to say what I want to—which is about Nick's expertise being a little too murdery. It's about solving crimes, not committing them. Tom is right behind her, his lips pressed so flat, they've disappeared.

Of anyone in this situation, he's going to have the hardest time reconciling the fact that we just killed half a dozen people like we were solving a Highlights for Kids picture puzzle.

"Yeah, we're done," Nick says, his eyes still on me.

Karrie blows out a breath. "Good. Let's get outta here. I do *not* want to get caught at the crime scene. And I really need to wash this—*hrmph*—blood off me."

Tom's lips roll in further. It's like his mouth has become a black hole that's sucking his face inward.

We all troop back to the car, but just before I get in on the passenger side with Tom moving around me to the back seat, he stops me.

"Thank you for keeping Karrie safe. And for not murdering me."

There is a seriousness to the tone that gives me the clue that he *knows*. I mean, he did just see me dispatch more than one mob goon, but that could be explained as a one-off necessity in saving his and Karrie's lives.

But he's thanking me for not murdering *him*, and I wonder for a second if it might be a veiled threat about turning me in.

No, I have to believe we're actually friends now. The fact that I only thought about killing him *once* for hurting Karrie is proof of that. Plus, he didn't turn Nick in, and that man's trail of dead bodies is a few miles longer than mine. He also knows it would devastate Karrie to lose me.

So if he's not actually threatening me, I decide to tease him with a threat of my own.

I take a breath and lean forward. "Let's hope I never have to."

His mouth drops open for a second, and I wink before lowering myself into the front seat.

Chapter Twenty-Three

A Story is Born

M y "told ya so" is the only thing keeping me from upchucking all over the damn place. Blood stains my sweater. Zack's face is speckled with it.

I close my eyes, breathing through my nose. When the metallic taste in my mouth has settled, I lean between seats until I can reach and pop the glove compartment. Inside—as expected, given Nick and Zoe—there are several packs of wet-wipes. I take one out, sniffing it first to clear the scent of blood from my nostrils before I hand it to Zack.

"Your face," I murmur.

He takes it, leans around the passenger seat headrest, and uses the rearview mirror to clean up.

A cruel sense of justice hits me as I watch him. Carlotta wanted to kill us. Kill us and put our friends behind bars.

A shudder rips down my spine. The wipe is suddenly too wet, almost sticky in my hands. I hurriedly get the last loose bits of easy-to-remove blood off my fingers and hurl the thing away.

"Hey," Zack turns to look at me, bits of blood still streaked across his tan skin. "You okay?"

I hesitate. Am I okay? I was just kidnapped, nearly killed, and my best friend is in a warehouse with a mobster cleaning up dead bodies. What the hell is my life?

"I, uh... I don't know. I've never been kidnapped before." I give half a chuckle, though my humor defense isn't working as well as I'd like.

"Well." Zack tosses his wipe on the floor of the back-seat as well. "As a veteran kidnappee, I can tell you this one wasn't great."

I raise an eyebrow. He settles a bit in his seat, reaching a hand out to me. I take it.

He pulls me close as he says, "There's the method. When that dickbag took me last year, I was unconscious for most of it. Definitely preferred."

I snort.

His chest dances with a chuckle. "Then there's the reason. Last time I was almost killed because you were falling in love with me."

I lightly slap his arm.

"And because I was already madly in love with you."

A smile creases my cheeks.

"This time," he continues with a sigh, "it was because I messed up a case and put the wrong person behind bars."

"Zack." My firm voice is soft. "You didn't put anyone behind bars. You helped make a case. The jury put Frank away for a multitude of crimes, child trafficking was just the most horrendous of them."

"Still." His voice cracks.

I pull away, turning to look up at him with wide, worried eyes.

He sniffs and shakes his head. "I've never been so wrong. And now the feds have their sights set on Nick and…" He clears his throat. "I can't stand the thought of something happening to him."

My cheek twitches up. "I get it. That's how I feel about Zoe." I pause, my brow furrowing. "And," I frown up at him, "you were pretty fucking wrong when you thought I was a black widow serial killer!"

"Was I?" He grins at me.

I sit up entirely, mouth shocked open. "I didn't sleep with and then murder men."

"No." His grin widens, eyebrows wiggling in a teasing way. "You slept with them, and then *Zoe* murdered them."

I huff out, "Okay, that's true."

Zack rubs his hand up and down my arm. We sit in a content, post-adrenaline quiet for a moment. Our friends do whatever serial killers and mobsters do to cover their tracks inside the warehouse.

A fresh jolt of adrenaline reminds me of the dangers we are still in.

I sit back. "What can we do to protect them?"

Zack's brow creases into a thoughtful and worried expression. He hesitates for a few seconds. Then, "The feds will be on Nick no matter what. Zoe knows how to scrub a crime scene," he grimaces slightly, "but Carlotta having someone kinda in her pocket with the FBI isn't good. They might look deeper into her death than we'd like."

"Do you have anyone besides Richards we can reach out to? Let them in on a few unofficial details that would keep Nick off *America's Most Wanted*?"

He nods slowly, already reaching for his phone. Carlotta and her goons left all our stuff in the crappy van they abducted us with. My phone is completely dead, but true to form Zack had his fully charged this morning.

"I think... gimme a sec."

I nod and pull away, thinking about what our next move is. None of us have an alibi for this morning. After Richards and the prison, all four of us go off the radar for a while.

My lips twitch into a frown. We need to get to the hotel. We need to clean up, get dressed, and go out. A late lunch by the river—somewhere with plenty of eyes. There's no way to verify whether a long walk along the water did or did not happen.

Though, we will need to get into the hotel through the service entrance. That won't be hard.

Part of my planning for this trip included making sure our hotel has road and alley access and checking the specs. There are cameras in the lobby and elevators, but that's it. As long as we stick to the stairwell and don't run into anyone on a shift, we should be good.

My thumping pulse eases a little at the knowledge that there is a plan to keep Zoe out of prison.

And Nick.

A grin splits my features. It's definitely too soon for them to move in together, but I can't imagine it will take long. Even with all the training Zoe has given me through the years, it's clear Nick meets and exceeds her cleanliness standards in ways that would–and do while he lives with us–drive me nuts.

A vision of the future slowly emerges in my mind's eye. Zack and me planning a wedding on the beach. Zoe complaining about wearing black while Nick stands beside her, laughing. The podcast continuing to grow—with a retraction and corrections about the Frank case. I think about the notebook of ideas I left in the hotel. It might be time to show it to Zoe—to share with her like she shared with me. And get her permission to actually write the whole story down.

My eyes get misty as I look at Zack. He's on the phone, firmly locking in vital information and a mound of un-verifiable bullshit with a name I recognize but don't know off the top of my head. Probably another contact he's mentioned in the past.

No kids.

I chuckle. We never discussed children. Not once. Zoe is the one who gets all gooey when we see little ones out and about. Despite her wrinkled nose at grimey hands and boogers, she thinks they're cute.

I see kids and wonder if they've had enough to eat. I wonder how thin the soles of their shoes are, where their parents are, if the front-facing way their guardians behave hides something sinister under the surface.

"Done," Zack says with a sigh of relief.

"Yeah?"

He nods. "After this is discovered," he gestures to the warehouse out his window, "it won't be difficult to get a warrant for Carlotta's residence. From there, I filled them in on what to look for."

I chew my bottom lip. "Will Nick have an issue with the rest of his family getting in trouble?"

Zack shrugs. "We have no idea how many of them were in on it with Carlotta. Besides, he was close with Stretch, but that was about it."

"The life of an enforcer?"

He nods. "It's hard to be good friends with someone you might have to pound to a pulp if they make a mistake. Even if that person is related to you."

I sigh. "I get not connecting with blood relations."

He snorts, then his expression gets serious. "Kar, I know you already said it, but we were also tied up and about to be murdered."

I raise an eyebrow.

"Are you sure you're okay with not having kids? No mini-goths running around a big house?"

"I'm so serious, Zack. I've *never* wanted kids." I huff a chuckle. "That's always kinda been Zoe's bag."

His eyes go wide. "Zoe? Miss Refuses-to-get-within-ten-feet-of-a-sneeze wants kids?"

My chuckle goes full laugh. "I don't know if she *wants* them. But she's always liked them more." I lean on his shoulder. "Besides, with Auntie Kar around, any future hypothetical children will absolutely be decked out as little goths."

It's his turn to laugh, and I feel the strain in him decompress.

My gaze catches on movement outside and I sigh.

"Speaking of Zoe," I murmur. "Do you think he'll come back to Spokane?"

Zack glances out the window. Nick and Zoe walk out of the warehouse at a leisurely pace. Smoke trails through the open door behind them.

I watch the two killers take little cloth booties off their shoes. Zoe laughs. I grin.

"You already have a plan, don't you?" Zack says, shaking his head with a bemused expression.

"It's entirely possible," I laugh. "Come on, we need to hurry them up."

A month later finds Zoe and me sprawled across my couch, tiny plates of mini quiche in hand and an open binder with perfectly organized tabs sitting on the coffee table. The weather is a balmy fifteen degrees, which has warmed her up considerably to a tropical wedding destination.

We've been at it for four hours, despite the fact that there will be a grand total of less than a dozen guests. Zack and I have zero desire to wait, as evidenced by the shiny black and silver ring already on my finger.

"And you're sure—"

"No vigilante shit during my destination wedding," I cut her off firmly. "Zoe, you cannot drop bodies on a well-documented vacation. You simply *cannot*."

She sighs, and I laugh. We've come to a compromise, because while killing people isn't technically a compulsion for her, it absolutely makes her happy. With Nick by her side, I'm less worried about them getting caught. Besides, it's important to share hobbies as a couple.

Their extracurricular activities also double as research for my *totally fictional* novel. Zoe's enthusiastic permission, combined with Zack's promise to help write the more gory bits, gave me the motivation I needed to actually type out my jumbled ideas.

Nick's weapons expertise has also helped, though he's wanting to hold off on reading much until it's done. He doesn't like spoilers.

"How are plans coming along?" the former mobster asks as he crosses from the kitchen door and plants a kiss on Zoe's forehead.

"They're going well," Zoe says with a smile. "Apart from the dress-code."

I roll my eyes. Nick laughs. Zoe lights up at the sound, and a warm ball of happiness spins with delight in my chest.

The first week home was stressful. Anxiety spiked with every phone call, every new alert, every mention of anything to do with Seattle. Eventually it eased.

Zack's chat with his secondary fed contact led to a full-blown investigation of Carlotta's house. The massive manor, inherited from Frank, carried mountains of evidence against both of them.

Not having an actual person to put in prison meant Nick couldn't turn state's evidence. Which means he doesn't have any kind of immunity. However, the documents in the Farelli house seemed to be lacking in a lot of the lower-level family members' information. He still needs to be careful, but constant searches of open warrants have yet to show anyone actively after him.

It helps that Richards was told to keep his investigation under wraps. Carlotta had the man so twisted around her finger that when the information got out about her being his informant, he got his ass punted down to black-lining documents in a basement somewhere.

"You about ready to go?" Zoe asks.

Nick nods. "I'm going to warm up the car, Edge."

I chuckle as he pulls on a heavy jacket and opens the apartment door. "You're such a passenger princess, you know that?"

Zoe laughs and starts packing up the multitude of pictures and papers on the table.

The kitchen door swings open and Zack strides over, a massive ceramic mug in his hands. Steam rises from the top, the scent of rich hot chocolate filling the living room.

"Here you go, babe." He passes me the mug, says bye to Zoe, and returns to cleaning up the dishes from brunch.

My best friend turns her crystal blue eyes on me, her immaculate brows raised with incredulity. "And you're a *princess* princess."

I raise my mug in a cheers. "You're damn right I am."

We laugh together. Loved, safe, and happy.

Then she gives me a quick hug and heads out to join Nick in the car. They've got to go give Mac some love before an evening trip to an unnamed city where a multiple-count convicted rapist has been recently paroled due to tainted evidence.

I set down my drink as the door clicks closed behind her. Pulling my laptop onto my thighs, I open it up and drag the mouse to the most recent saved document. With a sly grin, I open *Death of a Douchebag* and start writing.

EPILOGUE – NOT A MURDER, UNFORTUNATELY

SEVERAL WEEKS LATER

"There's sand between my toes," I complain.

Nick pats my hand, which is tucked into the crook of his elbow. "It will only be for the ceremony."

"But then there's the reception. I can't wash my feet in between. I'd have to walk through the sand to get to our room, and then I'd get *more* sand between my toes." I keep the smile plastered on my face because there's a photographer—courtesy of Griller and Doc. It's the only thing Karrie would let them pay for, though not for lack of trying on Griller's part.

We got around Karrie's hard line about the flowers by having me insist on paying, with Griller paying me back secretly. Since he's a plants guy, he inspected every black bloom that now spills over my free hand himself before the florist even laid them out. Then he arranged them *just so* before she could tie them up in the leopard print ribbon Karrie picked out.

I lost the argument about me wearing black as maid of honor, though I didn't push that hard. I'm just glad the only thing wrapped in leopard print is the bouquet. There'd been no argument about bare feet on the beach. That was just practicality and because everyone already knows my feelings about the matter.

Besides, today is not about me.

And yet Doc is smiling at me with a twinkle of tears in her eyes. But I think it's the sight of me next to Nick that has her feeling emotional even before Karrie comes into view.

To be fair, no one ever thought they'd see the day I'd be in love with anyone, let alone a man, but here we are.

Nick pats my hand again before we part ways so he can position himself on the other side of TCT while I stand next to the spot Karrie will soon occupy. I grimace as I stabilize my naked feet in the shifting sand, knowing the photographer has—thankfully—turned his attention to the figures standing underneath the tree that shades where the grass creeps at the edge of the beach.

Griller is beaming like the proud dad he is, and Karrie is smiling coyly as she meets Tom's eye.

I shoot a sharp glance in his direction to check his face, and it's exactly what I'd expect as he takes in the black lace number she's got on and the heavy black liner around her eyes. It makes them pop against her porcelain skin. I helped her make the lines crisp at the edges of her lashes, winging it just enough to give her the exotic look she wears so well.

The dress is gorgeous—the lace is laid over a nude colored fabric, so it looks like it's just a thin sheath of filigree along her sumptuous curves. It's a high-low style that bares her legs at the knee and falls in a long train behind her.

The sight of her draws my biggest smile, and I almost forget about all the unholy places I'm going to find unwelcome beach souvenirs.

The sun nestles into the crystal clear Caribbean waters as Tom and Karrie pledge their undying love to each other. Its light kisses the gentle waves with oranges and pinks in a splash of color behind them as they seal their love with a kiss of their own, and Tom abruptly drops her into a dip that has the rest of us whooping and hollering. The camera clicks a million times, and it's honestly like a scene from a magazine.

The scene that's not from a magazine is the one where some rando drunk person who's also staying at this resort stumbles into the reception and hands me their half-empty champagne glass so they can join the Cupid Shuffle.

Nick catches the look of homicidal rage and disgust that comes over my face and sidles up next to me, taking the glass and disposing of it before pulling out his never-ending supply of sanitary wipes.

"You can't kill Drunk Vacation Dancer," he says mildly, wiping first my hands then his own.

"I could," I point out, keeping my hands up while they dry like a surgeon about to enter the OR.

He smiles, leaning forward to kiss my cheek. "But you won't."

I glare at him and whine, "Cannoli!"

He ignores the nickname I pull out for special occasions only. Hey, this is a wedding—it counts. "Today is about Karrie," he reminds me. "And you promised no dead bodies on a well-documented vacation."

Those were, literally, the exact words, and my scowl deepens because I didn't cross my fingers behind my back.

"International crime gets messy fast," he adds. "And I didn't bring my booties."

I sigh heavily, shifting my gaze from Drunk Vacation Dancer (DVD, ha!) to Karrie, who's laughing as she bumps into Griller because that man cannot resist a good group dance but has no rhythm to speak of. TCT is talking with Doc toward the edge of the dance floor, but his eyes are locked on his wife, a depth of adoration in the gaze that warms my heart and melts my irritation.

Nick's arms slide around my waist, and I lean into him, visions of my own future dancing in my head. A future I never thought was possible for a little sociopath like me.

I turn in his arms to look up at him, fluttering my lashes while I pout like I've seen Karrie do a million times. "But we can go stalk some stalkers when we get home, right?"

He smiles down at me, a glint in his eye. "Anything for you, Edge."

A Love Note

Thank you so much for reading!

We appreciate the hell outta you. If you've enjoyed this book (and the first one), please consider leaving a review on Amazon, Goodreads, Barnes and Noble, or wherever you get your books!

As always, our families get this biggest shout out for their endless support. Notable mentions being to the spouses, who sometimes worry about our sanity and their safety.

Thank you to our moms for the quick read-throughs and feedback. Dana, Danielle, and Meredith—rockstar beta-queens! Thank you for reading and for providing valuable insights for the story.

From Tracey, a very special thank you goes to CH. Shiny, you're the motivating, kind, encouraging, protective friend that every girl needs in her life. Thank you for pushing me for more and for doing this with me. PSMFL!

Also by Tracey Barski

The Alternate Chronicles

The Alternate End of Cassidy Marchand
Resurrecting Cassidy Marchand
Cassidy Marchand Unraveled
Heart in Parallel

Compromised

Love Undercover

Written with C.H. Lyn

Secrets of the Unborn

ALSO BY C.H. LYN

The Old Tales
Song of the Deep
A Voice in the Tower
The Abredea Series
Hope and Lies
Truth and Fury
Miss Belle's Travel Guides
Lacey Goes to Tokyo
Damen Goes to Peru
Spooky Cat Stories
Spooky Cat
One Hell of a Road Trip
Spelling Disaster
Other Works with Tracey Barski
Secrets of the Unborn